SETH
OF THE
LION
PEOPLE

SETH
OF THE
LION
PEOPLE

Bonnie Pryor

MORROW JUNIOR BOOKS · NEW YORK

Copyright © 1988 by Bonnie Pryor
All rights reserved.
No part of this book may be reproduced or utilized
in any form or by any means, electronic or mechanical,
including photocopying, recording
or by any information storage and retrieval system,
without permission in writing from the Publisher.
Inquiries should be addressed to
William Morrow and Company, Inc.,
105 Madison Avenue,
New York, NY 10016.

Printed in the United States of America.
1 2 3 4 5 6 7 8 9 10

Library of Congress Cataloging-in-Publication Data
Pryor, Bonnie.
Seth of the Lion People / Bonnie Pryor.
p.   cm.
Summary: Although Seth, the young teenager with the twisted leg,
is only tolerated by his tribe for his storytelling abilities, he
senses his people are on the brink of a transition from hunters to
artisans and growers of food, if only he can become their leader.
ISBN 0-688-07327-1
[1. Man, Prehistoric—Fiction.   2. Physically handicapped—
Fiction.   3. Storytelling—Fiction.]   I. Title.
PZ7.P94965Se   1988   [Fic]—dc19   88-18747   CIP   AC

To everyone who searches
for that special place

Contents

SETH
OF THE
LION
PEOPLE

The People of the Lion

"Crooked Leg will make a fine wife."

Seth clenched his fists so tightly that his nails dug into his palms. He concentrated on the pain, hoping it would help him ignore the boys' taunts. Most days, Nar and his friends would have been with the rest of the Lion People, busy on the shady ledge outside the cave. But the heat of the late afternoon sun had driven them to the cool waters of the stream.

For a long time the four boys had been so absorbed

dunking and splashing one another that Seth had dared allow himself to hope that he would not be seen. He had forced himself to remain motionless, half-hidden by the tall grain growing along the banks. Without moving his head, he could see the cave that was home to his people. By day the wide ledge at the entrance was crowded. Here the women kept busy with their various duties while the men sharpened tools or shaped objects from wood. Now, though, it was almost evening, and most families were gathering to eat. The heavy scent of cooking meat filled the air, making Seth's stomach rumble with hunger, and still he did not move. He had hoped the boys would tire of their games and return for their meal. While he waited, his eyes followed the stream as it twisted through the rocks. From the cave, the stream cut through a small, wide valley— an easy walk, even for him. The valley was Seth's special retreat, a place where he could escape the scorn and pity of the others, if only for a short time.

Suddenly the wind shifted, flattening the grass, and one of the boys spotted Seth. Now Nar and his friends continued their games, occasionally pausing to jeer at him. Seth knew he should be used to their ridicule by now, as he had suffered through it for most of his life. It was Nar, the Leader's son, who was the worst. "Look at old One Leg," he sneered while Seth remained frozen by the stream. "He is only fit to do woman's work." Then he whispered something to the other boys, too low for Seth to hear, and they howled with laughter.

Although Nar counted thirteen summers, just like
Seth, everything else about them was different. Nar
reminded Seth of the bison who grazed in the valley
below the Lion People's cave. Like his father, Grunn,
he had a jutting chin that set off a perpetually scowling
face and cruel eyes.

With a rough barking hoot, Nar picked up a stone
and flicked it at Seth, looking back to watch his friends'
reaction. Seth would not give them the satisfaction of
showing his pain, although the stone had stung him.
Still, it had not hurt as much as the words. Perhaps
it was because they spoke the truth, Seth thought
bitterly. He rubbed at his twisted leg, broken in the
fall of rocks that had also killed his mother. Not a day
passed when he didn't fight the envy he felt at the
others' strong bodies.

Soon Nar and the other three boys Seth's age would
go on their first hunt with the men. They had been
training for it for a long time, first with weapons: spear,
ax, and a sling of leather for throwing stones. Then,
when their skill and strength satisfied the old men of
the tribe, they had been allowed to accompany the
hunters, but only to watch and learn. They had been
taught how to track, build a trap pit, and creep through
the grass with the wind at their faces so that even the
wily antelope would not catch their scent too soon.
Their games, too, prepared them for the day when
Marnak, the Keeper-of-Magic, proclaimed the signs
right for their passage into manhood. Once the hunt
was over, the boys would be permitted to sit by the

evening fire and be a part of the council of men. As part of the council, they would have a say in making the laws of the tribe, settling disputes, and deciding between war and peace with neighboring tribes.

Seth listened each day when the boys returned from their lessons, tired and dusty, but gloating with importance. He was certain he would never be accepted at the council fire. Nor could he believe that he would ever be called Leader, an honor that once might have been his and now seemed destined for Nar.

As Seth pondered his unfortunate fate, Nar and his friends suddenly ran off. This puzzled Seth until he saw his friend Esu and his father, Jon-tu, striding down the banks of the stream toward him.

"Are you hurt?" Jon-tu, the spear maker, asked kindly, watching the fleeing boys with a frown.

Silently Seth shook his head. He was ashamed that his humiliation had been observed.

With a short nod, Jon-tu continued up the well-worn path to the cave, but Esu lingered behind. Seth liked Esu, who never joined in the other boys' teasing, though now he hated the look of pity in his eyes.

"Why do you let them do that?" Esu asked. "You act as if you don't care. And why do you give them reason for their taunts by doing woman's work?"

Seth sighed. How could he explain to Esu that protesting was useless? It only made matters worse. Esu would not understand. With a strong young father and mother to protect him, he had never really known trouble. And as for the work, Seth found it peaceful sitting by the stream and guarding the grain from marauding animals. In fact, he had volunteered his help, much to the delight of the tribeswomen, who already had too much to do. Perhaps it had been easier for them when they only gathered the grain that grew wild in the valley. But since they had noticed that grain grew where the seed was dropped, they planted it in the narrow strip of land alongside the stream. The women did all this alone, because no man of the Lion People would lower himself to scratch the earth. Men were supposed to be hunters, and fighters if need be, although for many years now the tribe had known peace.

Still, Seth comforted himself with the knowledge that the grain was important. Many times, when the winter winds kept the hunters from success, it was the difference between life and death. At least, watching the grain, he felt of some use. But surely Esu would never understand.

Squatting in the dust beside Seth, Esu broke the silence. "You should leave. I myself would go with you. We could be traders. Think of the wonders we might see." Esu's eyes dropped to Seth's withered leg, and he gazed away in embarrassment.

"Look there," he shouted suddenly.

Seth was quick enough to see a flash of brown fur streak behind some rocks.

"A wolf," Esu said excitedly. "And so close to the cave! I should tell the hunters."

Seth shrugged. "It is far away by now." He looked

thoughtfully in the direction the wolf had fled. "The traders who came last summer spoke of people who made friends with the wolf."

"Surely you don't believe that," Esu said. "And even if it were true, Grunn would not allow it. 'The lion and the wolf do not sleep together,' " he said in a deep-voiced imitation of Nar's father that set both boys laughing.

Seth felt someone observing him, and he turned, expecting to see his tormentors again. Instead, it was his father, Magli. Seth wondered if he, too, had witnessed his recent shame. But Magli smiled. "It is time for your lesson."

Seth took after his father in his tall, lean build, though Magli's body was stooped now with age and sickness. Esu watched as Seth struggled to his feet and followed the old man to a huge tree, which was a comfortable distance away from the busy entrance to the cave. There Magli settled himself wearily under the spreading branches. Until two summers ago, Seth's father had been the Leader of the Lion People. Thanks to Magli, the tribe had spent the last few summers at the winter cave instead of moving to the summer hunting grounds. The council of men had discussed this idea for several winters, but it had been Magli who had made the final decision. And it had been a good one, too, Seth thought proudly. Ten young children and babies now proved the prosperity of the tribe. At the cave, the Lion People had gathered enough grain to keep them all winter. Not for many years had anyone gone to sleep hungry.

In the old days, the men of the tribe had fought for the position of Leader. But Seth's grandfather and Magli had been chosen by a vote of the council. Then Nar's father had used an old law to challenge Magli to a fight. When Grunn had won, he could have driven Magli and Seth away from the tribe. But Magli was loved, and since he was also the Teller-of-Stories, Grunn had reluctantly allowed Magli and Seth to stay. Fierce old Marnak, the Keeper-of-Magic, had been their greatest ally. "Without Magli's stories, the Lion People would soon forget the past," he had warned. "Then we would be no more than the animals grazing in the valley below. We would not remember the beginning of the world when the first men were given life by the sun."

Seth knew this story by heart. The first man had killed the lion, and when he had eaten it, he was suddenly filled with its spirit. The lion had given his people their strength, and also their name.

Esu stood back a respectful distance until Magli saw him and nodded his permission to listen. Seth tried not to notice the tired lines on his father's face. After his defeat, Magli had begun to wither, like a flower pulled up by its roots. Now his eyes were dim and his mind sometimes wandered. The oldest of the Lion People, he had lived forty-five summers, more than most men, and his body bore the scars of many hunts.

"I am afraid for you," Magli said to Seth at last. "I will die soon, for my bones ache and tell me this truth."

Seth turned away, not wanting to hear, but his father touched his face gently. "You must not be sad. I have lived a long life with the Lion People, and your mother, Nani, was a fine woman, even if she was not one of us. It was she who gave you your name. However, you must learn the stories quickly. They will be your protection when I am gone. As the Teller-of-Stories, you will always have a place."

"I am sorry to shame you. You should have a son who is a great hunter, one who could fight Grunn and make you Leader again."

Magli's eyes flashed with anger, and for an instant Seth thought his father would strike him, something that he had never done. But when Magli spoke, his voice was soft.

"You have been a good son. Your blood is strong, and the council would have supported you in spite of your leg. I lost you that right when I fought Grunn. I did not have to answer his challenge. I could have asked for a vote of the council, but I was too proud. Now he has surrounded himself with others like himself, and the rest of the council is too afraid to oppose him. There is even talk of returning to the old ways and following the animal herds to their summer pastures. But Grunn is not young, and his son is a bully. Who knows what might happen."

"They would never make me Leader," Seth said

hotly. "And if they did, I would not want it. The Lion People are not my concern."

Magli seemed not to hear. He started to speak, his voice hypnotic, holding the boys in his spell even though they had heard the stories many times before. "I was still a young man when we left the valley of the wild geese. Our cave was near a lake, and for many generations it had been our home. But a new people came. Their warriors were fierce, and they had many fine weapons. They raided our home, killing our men and taking the women and children to be slaves." Magli looked fiercely at his son. "Our own people have taken slaves in battle, but after a time, they become part of the tribe. Your mother was a slave, and I loved her no less because her people lived in houses of skins and bones. But the invaders to the valley did not accept slaves into their clan. My father was Leader then. It was he who began the journey to this place."

"Is that when Seth was hurt?" Esu spoke for the first time.

Magli nodded. "We stayed for a time by a river. It seemed a good place. Then the noise of our happiness woke up the mountain spirit. To show his displeasure at our presence, he made the earth shake and rocks tumble. Seth's mother was picking berries when it happened. She was killed, but her body protected our son. His leg was crushed, and for a long while I thought he would die, too. Even Marnak's magic was not strong enough to fight a mountain spirit. Finally Seth's leg healed, though it remained twisted and weak.

Esu gazed longingly across the distant hills. "I would like to have lived then. To have seen the world as you did. I can remember nothing but this place."

Seth smiled shyly at his friend. Although Esu was learning to hunt with the others, Seth knew his heart was different. Esu worked with his father, making tools. Although some of the hunters made their own, Jon-tu and Esu did such wonderful work that, more and more, others came to them. From bone, they also shaped scrapers and needles for the women and crafted fine beads and combs for trade. These Esu carved or decorated with colors. Wherever he went, Esu carried a small pouch to fill with materials for mixing colors. Sometimes he drew an animal on a rock just for Seth. They were so real, Seth almost expected them to spring to life.

Now, a twinkle in his eyes, Esu nudged Seth and nodded at Magli. While Seth had been lost in thought, his father's head had drooped. Beneath the tree, the gentle sound of Magli's snores filled the surrounding silence. Noiselessly, Esu left Seth at his father's side.

The Giant Bone

Seth did not see Esu much in the next few days, for his father was firm in his insistence that Seth practice his stories. "When I am gone, our people will depend on you to remember the past," Magli reminded his son whenever he complained.

Seth knew Magli was right. Yet he longed for the quiet coolness of the stream even while he repeated the Lion People's history over and over until his father was satisfied. At night, long after everyone else was asleep, the words still whirled in Seth's head.

Finally, one night, he conceded to wakefulness and sat up on his robe beside Magli to wait for the dawn. His sleeping place was near the wide opening of the crowded cave. Because it was damp, uncomfortable, and infested with fleas, the cave was usually empty by day. Now, by the dim light of the smoky stone lamps, Seth could see the ring of lion skulls around the entrance of the place his people called home.

Suddenly Seth jumped. The sky was filled with a faint rosy glow—he had nodded off, after all—and Esu was before him, touching his arm. His friend held a finger in front of his lips for silence and whispered an invitation. "Come with me."

Nodding, Seth glanced at Magli, still asleep, and pulled himself up painfully. After a night on the damp cave floor, his leg always ached. Even his warm robes could not keep out the chill. He stumbled over one of the hunter Sela's three small boys, but the child only sighed in his sleep.

Outside the cave, Seth found several of the women already busy preparing some hides before the heat of the day made work impossible. New hides were scraped and stretched until they were supple and smooth. Some of them were soaked in a dye of pigment and animal fat. Sewn into leggings, soft shirts, and shoes, the skins were comfortable and warm.

One of the women smiled at Seth and offered him a piece of flat, hard bread. He thanked her, though he winced at the look of pity in her face. Spotting Esu at the start of a nearby path, Seth hurried to catch up. Even as he hobbled painfully on his crooked leg, he could feel the woman's eyes on his back.

"Where are we going?" Seth asked when he reached his friend.

"It is a surprise," Esu said mysteriously. "I found something yesterday when we were practicing tracking. I couldn't stop then, but I marked the way. See there?" He pointed to a strip of bark peeled back from a tree.

After this cryptic explanation, Esu would not answer any more questions. Although he walked slowly, he still had to wait several times for Seth to catch up.

When the sun was quite high in the sky, they finally stopped to rest. "It's not far now," Esu promised, handing Seth a piece of meat to eat. Seth was nearly exhausted, and he was nervous. He had never been this far from the cave. What if they ran into a lion? Although most of the lions near the cave had been killed, sometimes a victorious hunter returned home with a pelt to add to his prestige. Even worse, Seth worried, what if they ran into other men? But Esu seemed unconcerned. He led the way through a narrow gorge, pausing now and then to check his markings.

"There," Esu said at last.

Seth gasped. They were standing in front of a sheer wall of rock. High above, Seth could see the sudden end of a flat plateau. The cliff wall was streaked with red, beautiful in the now bright sunlight. However, this was not the sight that had brought the gasp to his lips. Before him, on the floor of the gorge, lay a huge pile of bones. Seth had never seen so many bones in one place. In places, they were stacked higher than his head.

"I know what this is." He choked. "Magli has told me about it. For a long time, the Lion People have hunted by stampeding the animals until they fall off a cliff. Magli thinks it is a bad thing to kill so many when the people can eat only a few."

"Wait," Esu said. "Let me show you something even more amazing." Picking his way through the pile, he stopped in front of the biggest bone Seth had ever seen.

"What could have been so huge?"

"I don't know," Esu admitted. "But it looks very old. I want to take it home. A person could make many things with a bone such as this."

"Aaa-eee," Seth groaned. "I am sure you could make many things from such a bone. But tell me, my friend—how do you plan to get it home?"

Hands on hips, Esu considered the problem. "Surely the two of us can manage one bone."

"One bone, especially the one I see you drooling over, is bigger than us both. Perhaps you should have brought Nar. He could have used his strength for something besides throwing rocks at me." Seth intended the words as a joke, but they carried a bitter edge.

Esu clapped him on the shoulder. "I much prefer your company. And there is nothing wrong with your arms."

The matter was settled. With each shouldering one end of the treasure, the two boys started on the long walk back home. In places, Seth had almost to crawl to continue, but, stubbornly, he would not ask for a rest. After all, Esu had chosen him for the journey. As they neared the cave, he felt an exhilarating satisfaction that came out of his lips as a simple pattern of notes.

Esu looked surprised. "I like that sound. How do you make it?"

Seth showed him. "Pucker your lips. You can change the sound as you blow."

After several tries, Esu managed a weak note. "I did it!" he whooped with delight. "But you do it better."

"I have had more time to practice," Seth replied. "It is easy when you are alone." He hated the whiny sound of his voice.

By now the sun had nearly set, and Seth knew his father would be worried. So he was not surprised when Magli greeted him with angry words.

"Where have you been?" he demanded. "Some of the men have been out searching for you. We thought you might have been hurt or kidnapped." He stared at the boys' prize.

"I'm sorry," Seth mumbled.

"It's all my fault," Esu confessed as a crowd began

to gather. "I did not think it would take us so long. I wanted this bone to make something special."

Magli was impressed. "My father saw such a bone," he said thoughtfully. "He thought the first Lion People were giants. It is something to think about."

Pushing his way through the curious onlookers, Grunn sputtered, "Have you brought bad magic to our cave?"

"We found this at a place where hunters had stampeded animals to use for food," Esu protested. "There were many bones piled high."

"I have never seen such a thing. Perhaps it is as Magli says. Giants. There may be bad spirits inside that bone."

"Let Marnak decide," shouted Sela. There were shouts of agreement, and soon Marnak was examining the bone intensely. Without speaking, he sprinkled it with a few grains of color from the pouch he wore on a leather strap around his neck. Grunn shifted his feet impatiently, but Marnak would not be hurried. He studied the magic designs made by the color grains, walking carefully around the bone while Seth and Esu exchanged worried glances. Would they be forced to give up the reward for their day's work? But no. Marnak was smiling.

"I do not feel any spirits," he said. "The giant's spirits have already left, and the bone is cold."

Grunn gave an angry grunt and strode back into the cave, no longer interested. Esu looked pleased. Several of the younger children proudly helped him carry the bone to the place where Jon-tu worked. Now that Marnak had pronounced it safe, nearly everyone was eager to exclaim over the boys' find. Suddenly feeling his weariness, Seth waved at Esu and followed Magli back to the cave. Almost instantly he fell asleep, dreaming of mighty giants who walked the earth.

When he awoke the next day, he was surprised to see that it was so late in the morning. Nar and his friends had already left with Grunn and several other hunters. Some of the women were gone, too, probably to gather the last of the summer roots and berries. Near the cave entrance, a few small children played a noisy game. They stopped when they saw Seth and pestered him for information about the bone. For one day at least, the bone had made him a hero.

Seth found his father sitting in the shade of a twisted tree not far from the men and women working on the ledge outside the cave. Seth brewed Magli's morning tea, stirring in some of the healing herbs Marnak had given him.

"You have become good friends with the spear maker's son," Magli observed, sipping his drink.

"Yes, Father. He does not make fun of my leg."

"It is good to have a friend, especially one like Esu. He is young, yet he holds a certain position. It is whispered that his paintings are magic. I myself do not know if this is true. But the Lion People have enjoyed good fortune for many summers. The valley is rich with game, and no enemy has attacked for a long time,"

Magli said. "There are fifty-three Lion People, more than in most tribes. I counted them myself," he added proudly. "We have eight little ones of less than four summers."

"What does this have to do with me?" Seth asked. "I cannot make magic paintings."

Magli patted his arm and was silent for so long that Seth thought his father had forgotten the question.

"Our life is changing. Hunting is not the important thing it once was. As our tribe grows larger, we will need more land for the grain and a way to bring water to it. People will also want to live closer to the grain they grow instead of crowded together in this cave. Do you think Grunn or his son has the vision to make this happen? No. They want to lead us back to the old ways. Grunn's mind is closed. He thinks only of hunting and boasting. And his son is even worse."

"I still don't understand what this has to do with me, Father."

"The people need a good Leader." Magli waved his hand to silence Seth's protests. "There are those who would support you when the time is right. Jon-tu and Sela, for instance. And there are others. Think about it and learn all you can. Then, if the time comes, you will be ready."

Magli patted Seth's hand again. "Go now to your friend. I need more sleep. But remember what I have said." As Seth got up to leave, Magli's eyes closed and his breath became even and deep.

"Let's walk," Esu said when Seth found him on the ledge. "I have been working hard, and I need a rest."

"Doesn't it bother you to walk with me?" Seth asked. "Someone else could walk farther, and faster."

"Do you choose your friends for how fast they can walk? Can I not just like to be with you?"

"You are the only friend I have. I feel as if you are my brother," Seth said.

"Then that is what we shall be," Esu exclaimed. "We will make each other a promise. I will be your brother, and you will be mine." Esu drew a beautiful bone-handled knife from the pouch tied around his waist and made a tiny cut on each of their arms. Then he pressed his arm against Seth's. "Now our blood is the same, and we are brothers."

"I will make a story for this special day," Seth said. His voice was solemn, but suddenly he laughed. "Magli is going to be very surprised to learn that he has two sons."

"As will my parents." Esu chuckled.

Suddenly the laughter died from their lips. In front of them, only a few feet away, was the wolf the boys had seen before. It was a she-wolf, they could see now. She was lean, and her coat was covered with burrs.

Although he should have been frightened, Seth felt only pity. For in the wolf's eyes he read something he well understood. As the wolf slipped back into the trees and disappeared, he whispered, "I think she is lonely."

The Walking Stick

"A good teller-of-stories must know tales of every kind," said Magli a few afternoons later. "I am weary and need to hear something that will make me laugh."

"Long ago, the Lion People were not so many as now," Seth began hesitantly after a few minutes of thought.

His father nodded. "I am listening."

"The Lion People lived on the edge of a great water, and they were exceedingly happy except for one man named Bantok. Poor Bantok was already a grown man, ready to marry, but there were no young women in the clan.

" 'You must go out into the world,' Japet, his mother, told him. 'There are other Lion People beyond the mountain. Perhaps they have a daughter in need of a husband.'

"So Bantok made ready for his journey. But his mother was still not pleased. 'Bantok is a good son,' she said to her husband. 'He is kind and brave, and he is even a little handsome. But, aaa-eee, I know that he is also very foolish. I worry that I will never be called Grandmother. However, if he can find a proper wife, I will not have to cook and sew until my old bones are tired. Perhaps I should go with him and help him select a suitable girl.'

" 'A man cannot bring his mother to help him pick a wife. I will go with him,' said Bantok's father. In truth, he was glad to escape his wife's nagging tongue.

"The next morning, Japet packed some dried meat and berries in a pouch and sent her husband and son off on their quest."

Magli nodded. Seth's skills as a storyteller grew stronger as the story unfolded. Magli could hear the voices of the crafty wife, the weary husband, and the eager son. Some of the other Lion People drifted closer to listen.

"Bantok and his father traveled for many days, and

at last they found the mountain people. 'We have come for a wife,' said Bantok's father.

" 'It happens that we have two daughters,' said the mountain Leader.

"Bantok and his father laid out the gifts they had brought: furs, salt, and shells. The Leader was pleased. In his clan, it was the custom for the bride to pay the husband. But he said nothing of this to the strangers. Still, he loved his daughters and wanted to make sure Bantok would make a proper mate.

" 'Stay for a while and work,' said the father. 'If you help out well, surely you may have a bride.'

"So Bantok and his father stayed. Never did a man work harder than Bantok, for he had seen the lovely Lela, and her laughter fell like gentle rain on his ears.

"At last the girls' father called Bantok to his side. 'You have done well. Tomorrow we will have a wedding feast, and you may take Setep back to your clan.'

" 'But it is Lela I want,' cried Bantok.

"The father shook his head. 'Among my people the oldest girl must marry first.'

"Aaa-eee," Seth continued. "Poor Bantok. He had seen the daughter Setep, and although she was as pretty as her sister, she had a sharp tongue like that of his own mother. Bantok's father was even more worried. If I bring this girl home, we will never have peace at the hearth fire, he thought. So that night he paid a visit to his promised daughter.

" 'We are glad to take you into the family,' he said.

'And I hope my son will not beat you too hard.'

" 'Beat me?' asked Setep in alarm.

" 'Oh yes,' said the father. 'It is a custom of our people. Each wife must be beaten every day. But perhaps if you do your work well, my wife will ask her son to be gentle. She is eager to have a girl do everything for her.'

" 'I must do all of her work and my own?'

"When Bantok's father nodded, Setep thought of a plan. All the young men like Lela more than me, she told herself. Yet she has eyes for the young stranger. If she were gone, I could have my pick.

"At the feast the next day, the father of the bride was surprised to see his daughter wrapped in a deerskin, her head bowed low. Bantok's father spoke quickly. 'It is the custom of our people for a bride to cover her face at the marriage ceremony.'

"The Leader of the mountain people bade his daughter good-bye, and the travelers started the journey home. Imagine Bantok's pleasure when the skin was lifted and he found his new bride was Lela, the one he loved."

Seth's audience nodded and chuckled appreciatively. "What of Bantok's mother?" asked Esu, who was among those listening. "Was she pleased with the new wife? Did it soften her tongue?"

Seth grinned. "Lela proved to be as clever as she was beautiful. When Japet ordered her to cook the meals, Lela smiled sweetly and said, 'Oh, Mother, you do it so much better. Please show me once more so that I might learn.' And when Japet told her to scrape and stretch the hides again, Lela would sigh, 'I shall never make skins as soft as you, Mother Japet.' In this manner, the two women worked together. And later, Lela presented her with so many fine fat grand-children Japet had no time for grumbling. She and her husband stayed at the hearth fire of their son and lived out their days in contentment and peace."

"Well done," Magli said, smiling.

That evening, Esu handed Magli a bowl of steaming stew. "My mother made this for you," he said. "She flavored it with special herbs, since our salt is nearly gone. It is good, but I wish we could find a salt cave. We always run out before the traders come."

Magli chewed slowly. Seth knew his father was growing weaker. He slept most of the time now, and even eating seemed to tire him. "Tell your mother we thank her," he said to Esu, picking out the tender pieces of meat with his fingers. "It is delicious."

The boys finished their own meal and waited politely until Magli had finished his. Almost immediately, the old man dropped off to sleep.

"I have something for you," Esu whispered. "It is a present. Come and see." He led Seth back to his father's workplace. From under a skin he pulled out a long, carved stick. It was so long Seth knew it could have been made only from the giant bone they had found. One end of the stick was smoothly forked, and the sides were decorated with running deer.

"It is a thing of great beauty," Seth said slowly. "But what is it for?"

Esu grinned. "Here, my not so smart brother. Let me show you."

He placed the forked end under his arm and used it to propel himself forward. "Now do you understand? It is a new leg. You will be greater than everyone, for now you have three legs instead of only two."

"It is wonderful," shouted Seth as he hobbled about. A slow grin spread across his face. "Aaa-eee. It is like magic."

Hearing Seth's gleeful cries, many tribespeople stopped to watch and admire the walking stick. Seth agreed with their exclamations of "ohh" and "ahh," for Esu's gift was truly a thing of great beauty as well as useful. He was surprised to realize that he had become, at least for the moment, a person of importance. Even Nar seemed impressed, although his eyes tightened with jealousy. And Mara, so pretty and shy, smiled at him before her mother called her away.

The sun was setting, and a cool breeze that smelled of autumn ruffled the dying fires. Eager to prolong his moment of glory and repay his friend, Seth began a story for the men, women, and children gathered outside the cave.

"Today the hunters stampeded many horses off a cliff," he began. "So many died that most of the meat could not be carried, and it was left for hungry scavengers." Far off in the distance the eerie song of wolves sounded in the night, and Seth paused. "Our people have always done this, and in another place the bones are piled as high as a man's head." Glancing at Grunn, who was scowling faintly, Seth took a deep breath before continuing. He had been thinking about the ghastly pile of bones since the day he saw it. "Perhaps this way of hunting is not such a good thing," he continued bravely. "Think about the days when our hunters return with empty hands."

There was an uneasy rustling among the listeners, and Grunn's frown grew deeper. Seth knew he was on dangerous ground, and he turned the story with happier words.

"Out of all this death, Esu, the brother of Seth, made a wonderful thing. On it he carved running deer to make it swift, and he gave it to his brother. Seth was alone, walking slowly with only one leg, but now he will run like the deer, fast and strong on his three legs." Almost everyone was smiling now, and Seth gave his story life, moving his body in an imitation of his old shuffling walk, and at last running smoothly with the aid of the stick.

He kept his audience entertained with other stories: tales of heroes and cowards, sad times and funny times. He talked until his voice became hoarse, and when he had finished, he knew he would be accepted in his father's place. As the group readied for sleep, the hunter

Sela clasped Seth's arm. "Well done, Teller-of-Stories. And you are right about the hunt. There is no honor in such killing."

Not all were so pleased. Grunn stomped away without a word, and several of his hunter friends muttered in anger among themselves. Nar was even more outspoken. "Stick to your stories, Crooked Leg," he hissed. "Leave the hunting to us men."

Briefly, Seth worried. Did he have the right to criticize what he himself had never experienced? But his joy over the walking stick and his evening's success overcame any doubts.

When the boys discovered a hidden patch of berry bushes the next morning and were stuffing their mouths with handfuls of the purple goodness, Seth noticed the she-wolf watching them from a high bluff. He saw her often now, and he wondered again about her. Wolves traveled in packs, yet she was always alone. In an odd way, he felt drawn to her. Although he feared her strength, he sensed a need that matched his own.

Suddenly Seth and Esu stiffened. An unfamiliar smell alerted them to the strangers nearby. As the men passed only a few feet away from the berry thicket, they spoke quietly to one another in a language that Seth and Esu did not know. All thoughts of eating vanished. As soon as the strangers were gone, the boys took a different path back to the cave, reaching it only minutes before the men arrived.

"Strangers!" Esu shouted. Instantly the camp was

abuzz with activity. Spears were grabbed and children herded to the dark protection of the cave. The Lion People watched anxiously as the foreigners approached. Seth and Esu stood with the hunters. Curiously, Seth noticed, Nar was not there. Perhaps, Seth thought unkindly, Nar was only good at fighting someone who could not strike back.

When the four men emerged from the woods, they held up their hands in a gesture of friendship. Prudently, though, they waited some distance away until Grunn, lion skin over his shoulders, strode out to meet them.

Suddenly the apprehension changed into excited murmurings. They were salt traders from the land of the big water! Grunn escorted them proudly, as though he personally was responsible for their visit. Seth and Esu choked back giggles at his pompous strutting. It seemed ludicrous in such a shaggy bear of a man.

Although the traders spoke only a few words of the Lion People's language, by gesturing they were able to make themselves understood. With great ceremony, they displayed their goods: salt, shiny beads of blue-green that brought sighs of pleasure from the women, and nuggets of copper and shells.

The women looked hopefully at the men, but they waited, as was customary, for Grunn to make the first bargain. Finally, with a great flourish, he offered a lion skin. Clearly the traders were impressed. Only the greatest hunters killed such a beast.

Esu's father, Jon-tu, traded next. He offered scrapers and needles in return for a nugget and some beads.

After the trading was over, the storytelling began. One of the traders told of a place with many people. A town, he called it.

"More people than this?" Grunn asked, indicating the Lion People.

"Many more," another assured him. "The people live in huts they have built themselves," he explained. "And they keep goats in a fence made of thornbush."

"What a wonderful idea," Seth exclaimed, unable to contain his enthusiasm.

Grunn's eyes narrowed. "The men must be poor hunters if they have to fence in the animals. And to make houses! What a lot of useless work. Their leader must be very weak if he can't find a good safe cave."

Passionately, Seth spoke again. "But if we lived in houses, we could live closer to the grain and grow more of it. And fencing in the animals would protect us from hunger after a poor hunt."

Although several men of his tribe gave Seth a warning look, he saw even more look thoughtful, as though they agreed. Grunn's face became red with anger.

"That is a bold speech for a boy who has not seen the ritual of manhood. It is only through my great kindness that you and your father are not outcasts, fit only to be food for the dog. But I will do you another kindness and explain why your idea is foolish. In the cave we can protect our people. We are together, one face turned to an enemy. And to keep animals would be an insult to the spirits. What animal would allow us to hunt it if it saw its brothers penned up like slaves? You see, little one," Grunn said in a softly mocking tone, "that is why I am Leader. It is like looking at a spear. I can turn it in my hand, seeing all sides, the whole truth of these matters, while you see only the edge."

Although Seth could think of a hundred more arguments, he wisely bowed his head. "I am sorry. I had no right to speak in such a manner."

His good humor restored, Grunn ignored the puzzled looks of the traders and ordered Seth to entertain with a story.

Seth's mind raced. He must choose wisely. He knew his tale must show the glory of the Lion People to impress the traders, who would carry the news to others. He also knew that in challenging Grunn, he had created a dangerous enemy. He had to make amends for that as well.

"Grunn, the greatest of all hunters, killed a lion with one thrust of his spear," he began. "It was not an old lion. It was a young, strong male, with teeth like knives." As he slowly wove the tale, the traders listened with rapt attention. Seth's arms moved with signs so that they might better understand. His voice roared with the thunder of the stormy night when the lion stalked the hunters taking shelter from the storm. His voice grew soft as he described how Grunn's early morning walk to the river had been interrupted by the lion's attack. When the story ended, there was a collective sigh of pleasure, and Grunn smiled benevolently as the men exclaimed over his skill and bravery.

"A wise Leader knows when to keep silent," Magli scolded Seth when he returned to the cave later that night. Seth's father had been too weak to attend the feast, although he had listened from his bed.

"I am not Leader," Seth mumbled, knowing his father spoke the truth.

"You cannot help it." Magli softened. "Your thoughts are wise. Do you intend to swallow those thoughts and let the Lion People live in darkness while the rest of the world learns new ways? A man does not have to be called Leader to teach new ways."

"I owe nothing to the Lion People," Seth said bitterly. "All my life, most of them have taunted and pitied me. Even now, though they like my stories, I am not really accepted. Do they ask me to join the council? Will I ever be offered a wife? I am tolerated because I am the storyteller, but I will never be truly one of them."

"Who knows what tomorrow will bring," Magli said. "You share the Lion People's blood. And not all have been unkind. What of Jon-tu's family? And there are others. They will support you when it is time. They are afraid of Grunn for now. But people will live only so long under the hand of a bully."

That night, his father's words repeated in his mind,

and Seth could not sleep. He heard the traders leave with the first rays of dawn. The excitement continued that morning when Marnak, the Keeper-of-Magic, announced, "Last night the lion spirit came while I was alseep. He showed me a valley full of bison, so that the earth shook with their passing. The dust rose to the sky, and when I looked again, the lion had killed. One, two, three, they fell wounded by the terrible teeth. It is the sign at last."

"Aaa-eee," went up the joyous cry. Today boys would become men.

Tȝe Hunt

Gleefully bragging and joking, the would-be men made preparations for the hunt. In the midst of this early morning excitement, Esu came to Seth. "This must be a hard day for you, brother."

Seth tried to look happy, waving away his friend's sympathetic glance. "I will share in your triumph," he said. He did not tell Esu of the idea that had sprung in his mind the day he received the magic stick. He could follow the hunters. If he could see the hunt, smell the scent of animals and men, and feel the tension, he thought, these things could make up in some small way for his loss.

When the men, ready at last, headed down the hill, Seth's heart pounded with excitement. A few of the women gave him understanding looks before they returned to their work. Seth waited for as long as he could before edging his way to the trail that would take him to the broad valley below the cave. He looked back to see if anyone was watching. But no one noticed that he was gone, not even Magli, still asleep on his skins.

Later that day, Seth climbed a small hill and gazed with dismay at the freshly trod but empty path. He had followed the hunters' route since morning as it twisted and turned through rocky and heavily forested land, but he was falling farther and farther behind.

Now he had completely lost sight of the men and boys, and he wasn't sure he knew the way back. *Crack!* snapped a branch behind him, and Seth jumped. But it was only a rabbit, frozen with fear.

"Go on." Seth chuckled. "This is your lucky day. It is only I, the Teller-of-Stories, and not a mighty hunter."

The rabbit dived into the brush, no doubt amazed to find itself alive. Seth leaned on his stick and searched again for his tribesmen.

From his vantage point, he could see the huge valley below, nearly flat and thick with a growth of tall grass. Behind him, toward home, rose the foothills. Beyond the cave, these became jagged mountains, hidden in a bluish mist.

Searching the valley, Seth spotted only a herd of bison grazing peacefully in the midday sun. The hunters must be nearby, he knew with certainty. But they were invisible, hidden by the tall grass. Using his stick for support, Seth slid down to a sitting position. With a sigh, he settled back against a boulder to wait.

He watched an old bull raise his head, sniffing nervously. Suddenly the animal pawed the ground, bellowing a warning. Then Seth saw the hunters, slipping through the grass to close the circle. With one mind, the animals began to run. While most escaped, it was too late for others. Faintly, Seth could hear the triumphant yells that accompanied the flying spears. This night there would be a magnificent celebration. This night no one would sleep with hunger.

Once Seth thought he saw Nar, leaping in a frenzied dance of glee, and another time he thought he saw Esu. It was difficult to pick out faces at this distance and with the great cloud of dust rising lazily to the sky. The thick dust reminded him that it had been a long time between rains. If the land became too dry to grow grass, he wondered, would the animals move away? That would force the Lion People to choose between hunger and abandoning their home. Grunn believed their lives were guided by the spirits who ruled the land. Yet the traders had described a people who fought hunger. It was a good idea, Seth thought, to keep some animals close to home, no matter what Grunn said about spirits. If you always had food nearby, who would care if the hunting was bad?

The traders had said there were many people living in the town. That probably meant their young did not die of hunger, as sometimes happened to the Lion People. Seth wished he could see the animal keepers and judge for himself.

While he had been distracted by these thoughts, the hunters in the valley below had tied the fallen bison, hacked into manageable pieces, to poles. With Grunn in the lead and Nar directly behind, the men rested the poles on their shoulders and began the journey back to the cave. They would travel directly beneath Seth, through a narrow passage on the trail. He did not want them to see him, but if he climbed down now, they would. Rubbing his aching leg, he closed his eyes and rested until it was safe for him to follow.

Suddenly he awoke to a squeal of rage. Using the boulder for support, Seth pulled himself up. He saw the men through a sleepy fog, but he understood instantly that this was not a dream.

Grunn was partway through the passage, looking helplessly on as a wild boar charged directly at Nar. The boar was a huge one, and his tusks were wickedly curved. Seth watched Nar, rooted in terror, and heard his cries of pain. Without taking time to aim, Seth grabbed his spear and threw.

The weapon flew straight and true, hitting the beast in one eye just as it turned to attack again. With a single short squeal, the boar dropped to a shuddering halt. Still screaming, Nar held his leg, and Seth could see bright red blood squeezing between his fingers.

By now the others had caught up. Several ran to help Nar, and then someone pointed to the cliff where Seth remained standing, unable to comprehend what he had done.

"It is the Teller-of-Stories," one of the men yelled.

Two of the hunters charged up the hill. Grabbing Seth, they carried him back down, shouting his praises. Soon Esu was next to him, pounding on Seth's back, grinning. "Today we are all men."

"What a story you can tell now," someone teased.

Grunn pushed his way through the throng. "It was a fortunate throw," he acknowledged grudgingly, though Seth saw there was no gratitude in his eyes. "But he cannot be counted among the men. This boy did not take part in the hunt, nor has he learned with the others."

There was an unhappy murmuring. "He did not need the practice." "It is a magic day."

Suddenly Marnak appeared before Seth with appeasing words. "It is a sign. This boy was meant to sit at the council fire. The spirits have chosen him with the others."

In such matters, Marnak's word was law. Grunn nodded grimly. "So it shall be," he said, flashing Seth a hateful look before turning back to his son.

I have shamed him and Nar, thought Seth. He was amazed by the hunters' continuing enthusiasm. They seemed determined to make him a hero. Indeed, since Esu had given him the walking stick, everything in his life seemed to have changed. Perhaps the walking stick was magic, or perhaps he himself had changed. It was something to think about.

Meanwhile, Marnak packed Nar's leg with mud and leaves to stop the bleeding. "It is bad, but it will heal in time," he announced. After a rough litter was fashioned from branches and a skin, the journey back to the cave began again. Seth watched Nar's face, wondering if he would see a reflection of Grunn's malice in his son. It was there, but there was something else as well. Perhaps a grudging respect? Seth saw it for only a moment before the wounded young man closed his eyes.

If Nar had felt any gratitude, it was gone by that evening. At the celebration, he huddled next to his father, pale and miserable. But Seth, who could never have imagined such a day, was steeped in glory. One by one, the newly made men were honored and each kill was reenacted. Sometime before dawn, Seth stumbled back to the cave to check on his father.

Magli was awake. "To injure the pride of a man like Grunn is a dangerous thing," he said weakly. "Do not give him any more cause for anger."

"I will be careful," Seth assured him. He sat at Magli's side until the old man was asleep again. The first pale streaks of light were already breaking in the eastern sky, yet Seth could still hear the shouts and laughter from the circle of men. Even so, he did not return to the celebration. He wanted time by himself to think. So much had happened this day. Following the stream, he walked away from the cave alone.

The she-wolf was drinking near Seth's special spot, the place where he had gone for solitude when he was merely a frightened and bitter boy. Was it possible that only a few short weeks had passed since the day Nar had thrown the stone?

With the early morning breeze in his favor, Seth was able to watch the she-wolf for some time without being detected. Then the touch of autumn chill gave him away. Sensing Seth's shivers, the she-wolf looked up at him.

"Today I am a man," he told her. "A hunter like you." He wasn't sure why he spoke to her. Of course she did not understand. Maybe he was made bold by the spear he held in his hand, the spear that had made such a difference in his life. Or maybe it was because he imagined, in that brief second before she fled, that her eyes had flashed with recognition. Surely he only thought he saw her look of longing. But in his heart, as he walked homeward, he knew it had been there.

All that day, he thought about the she-wolf, even while he worked with Esu and Jon-tu. Jon-tu was teaching him how to chip with the special rock, striking it so that long, slender flakes broke from the sides.

"You have a good hand for this," Jon-tu said. "I am glad for the help. My son, Esu, would rather dream or carve." He patted his son fondly as he spoke.

"I would never be as good as you," Seth said, embarrassed but pleased.

"If we made enough, we could travel with them like traders," said Esu.

Jon-tu laughed, and Seth smiled. These days, Esu and his father filled an empty spot in his heart. Magli did little now but sleep, and Seth missed their long talks. He wished Magli would be well soon.

But Magli did not get better, and as autumn passed into winter, Seth spent more and more of his time at his father's side, watching while the old man slept.

In spite of the fortunate hunt on magic day, the meat for the tribe did not last long, and later hunts were not so successful. Once winter struck in full fury, the summer herds were gone until the warm weather returned. Too often, all the Lion People had to eat was dried berries and flat bread.

The cold was worse than usual that year. Bitter winds whistled through the cave, overpowering the sticks and skins piled in front of the entrance. Still, it was warmer inside, although smoky from the many hearth fires. And restless, screaming children frayed already shortened tempers.

By now Nar's leg had healed and he had reverted to his bullying ways. Seth, however, was not his frequent target. And Esu gleefully reported discontented rumblings inside the cave.

"They say that Grunn is getting old, and Nar should not be Leader. Some of the men even think that the council should choose the next leader. I am sure it would be you. The men say you have good ideas for one so young."

But Seth was too worried about Magli to listen to

such gossip. Magli was racked with coughs, pale and wasted. It was plain he would not see the spring.

"You must get well," he begged one night, futilely forcing broth between his father's lips.

Weakly, Magli pushed the wooden cup away. "I will die soon."

"Where will you go when you die?" Seth whispered helplessly.

"No one knows. Perhaps we go back to the sun who gave us life. Perhaps to another world where only the dead live. You will be strong and take my place. Through you I will live." Magli was silent so long, Seth thought he had fallen asleep. But suddenly his eyes opened, and he grasped Seth's arm. "You will tell my story at the council fire?"

When Seth nodded, Magli smiled. In the morning, without speaking again, Magli was gone.

It was then Seth discovered how much Magli had been loved by the Lion People. As the men carried his father's body to the place of the dead, the keening of the women filled the cave. Marnak painted Magli's body with red ocher, symbolizing the blood of life, and a necklace of lion teeth was placed on his head so that all who saw him in the next life would know he had been a mighty hunter. Near his body were gifts to aid him on the journey to the place of the dead: a knife, a scraper, some beads, and a pouch filled with precious salt for trading. Then men and women both recounted Magli's life for his son to use against the pain in his heart.

Friend

The mourning continued for days before life returned to normal and Seth was left alone with his pain. Only Esu and his family did not forget. "You are welcome to a place at our fire," Jon-tu said one morning.

Seth considered his answer. "I am grateful. But I need time by myself."

"Take your time," Jon-tu said gravely. "Come when you are ready."

Seth stumbled away from the cave. The snow was

thick, and a thin crust of ice had formed on top, making it difficult to walk. He staggered and fell. Unable to move, he cried in grief and fear.

Slowly his sobs died away, and Seth became aware of the smell of wet fur and wildness. The hairs of his neck prickled with warning, and he sat up, furiously rubbing his eyes. If he was to die here alone, it would not be with red eyes, like a child. As he raised his arm, Seth heard a low throaty growl that made him freeze. Only his eyes moved, searching the bush until he saw the she-wolf crouched on a rock a few feet above. Fear made him sweat in spite of the cold, and his hand snaked out, feeling for a rock.

He met the she-wolf's eyes and he spoke. "You may kill me, wolf. But it will not be without a fight."

Seth watched the animal's ears cup toward his words. He thought her eyes looked curious, and something else—something he had felt the last time. Lonely. Like him, she was alone.

Very slowly, Seth rose to his feet. "Perhaps we are the same," he went on, "you and I. I, too, have no family."

Still the she-wolf sat, as if frozen. Seth allowed his hand to relax on the rock. He was less afraid now, but still wary. When he spoke to her again, he thought that the sound of his voice seemed to calm her.

"You do not look like a wolf. Your hair is brown and you are small. Is that why you are alone, because you are different? That, too, is something I understand."

Suddenly she rose, her neck hair bristling. As she lowered her head, her lip curled back and she growled fiercely. Seth tightened his hold on the stone. He felt a pang almost like betrayal. Why had she chosen now to attack? Then he realized that she was looking not at him but at the pathway directly behind him. Hearing the soft crack of a dried twig, he whirled around. "No," he roared.

Startled, Esu stood with his spear still poised for a throw.

"It's a wolf. She will kill you," he said as though Seth were a child he was instructing. Then slowly he lowered his arm.

Seth turned back, but the wolf was gone. A sadness washed over him. Just for a brief moment he had understood what it would be to call such a beast friend.

"She might have killed you," Esu repeated.

"I don't think so," Seth answered. "I think she understood my feelings."

"She was probably trying to decide whether to have you for breakfast or dinner," Esu joked. His look made it clear that he thought Seth's behavior was most peculiar. Awkwardly he touched his friend's arm. "My father sent me after you, to bring you back. We were worried."

Esu helped Seth over the icy patch of snow, and they returned to the clan. But the next day and for many days afterward, he found time to slip into the forest and leave an offering of meat on the rocks where he had seen the creature. Each day the gift from the day before would be gone. Of course, Seth did not know if it was the wolf or another hungry forest animal who took it. He knew that Esu's family could not really spare the meat. Sometimes he tried to eat less to make up for the loss, but that only provoked worried looks from Esu's mother and father.

One morning the wolf reappeared on the rocks. As before, she sat some distance away from him.

"I knew I would see you again," Seth said softly. "We are going to be friends. You know it, too, don't you? That is what I will call you. Friend. It is a good name, don't you agree?"

For the next several weeks, the she-wolf cautiously eyed Seth whenever he came to the forest. Despite Seth's coaxing, she always kept a few feet between them. Then one day Esu slipped quietly beside Seth as he was talking to her. At his approach, Friend retreated, but soon returned, watching warily.

"She comes every day now," Seth whispered. "I think she trusts me a little. But she still will not let me touch her."

"I knew you were up to something. Forgive me for following. I missed you." He gave Seth a lopsided grin. "And I have to admit I was curious."

"I was going to tell you. I wanted it to be a surprise."

Esu shook his head. "It is trouble, brother. The Lion People have always hunted wolves and wild dogs. Grunn will not like this. He will say wolves drive away the game."

Seth refused to think of unpleasantness. For now it

was enough that with Friend he felt truly happy. And the abrupt end of the harsh winter made it easier to avoid Grunn and his son. Almost overnight, the air had become sweet with the scent of new leaves and flowers. Quickly the skins were rolled back from the cave entrance, and the Lion People emerged like bears after a hibernation.

With the warm weather, Esu and Seth were able to spend more time away from the cave. One memorable spring day, the boys lay sprawled on their backs, watching the clouds change shape.

"Look at that one." Esu laughed. "It reminds me of Grunn. See? It is even frowning."

Seth laughed, too, then muffled the sound when he spotted Friend approaching from the woods.

"It is all right," Seth said soothingly. "Come here. I have something for you to eat."

The she-wolf crept nearer while the boys held their breath. It was as close as she had ever ventured. At last she stretched out and accepted the meat from Seth's hand. As she did, Seth brushed her neck, still shaggy with winter fur.

Suddenly Friend jumped away, a low growl in her throat. There was someone on the path. Seth twisted around in time to see a shape hurry through the trees. "Did you see who it was?" he asked Esu.

"It was Nar," Esu said unhappily. "He is sure to tell his father now."

Seth tried to make light of his worry. "Grunn will

never catch Friend. She is too smart. Unless," he added, frowning, "she can't leave."

"What do you mean?" Esu asked.

"Well, she may not want to leave. Did you notice that she was heavy with milk? I think she has had pups. They must be nearby."

"So that's why she was bold enough to take the meat from your hand."

Seth nodded. "I hope the pups are well hidden," he said.

"It would be nice if we could find them," Esu added. "When you first tried to tame Friend, I thought you were crazy. But seeing you with her has made me change my mind. Think how much easier it will be to make friends with a young one."

"Wolves are wonderful hunters. What if we could train them to hunt for us?" Seth asked suddenly.

"If we could do that, not even Grunn could object," Esu agreed excitedly. He gave Seth an admiring look. "My father is right. He says the spirits fill you with wonderful ideas. Aaa-eee, what a great leader you would be."

Seth shook his head. "Magli said a good leader never tells people what to do. He gives them ideas and then they must decide. You can see," he added bitterly, "what they have decided. They would rather have a leader who grunts like a wild pig."

"They are afraid of Grunn."

"How can they expect me to stand up to him when

all the strong hunters cannot?" Seth said, struggling to his feet. "And I am not sure I would want to be Leader even if I could. My life is not so bad now. I am accepted as the Teller-of-Stories, and I have a few friends. It is enough. If I could find a way to have Grunn accept Friend, I would even be happy."

"Then we should try to find the pups," Esu said firmly. "If we could train them to hunt, we could ask the council to vote for our keeping them."

"They would have to vote against Grunn," Seth said hopelessly. "And Friend may not let us near the pups."

"We can go slowly, a little closer each day," Esu suggested.

"That might work," Seth said, his interest renewed. Then a frown crossed his face as he remembered Nar. "We will have to be clever. Each day we must leave the cave by a different route. Then, when we are sure Nar is not trailing us, we can circle around to the woods."

Filled with their dreams, the boys hurried homeward. They didn't see the girl until she stepped through the bushes at the edge of the path near the cave. It was Mara, the daughter of Ali and the prettiest girl in the tribe. Her mother was the widow of a hunter killed the year before by a wild boar. Ali was bitter over her husband's death, grumbling sourly day and night until most people avoided her. Seth felt sorry for Mara, who had no way to escape her mother's acid tongue. It was no secret that Ali intended for Mara to marry Nar someday. As the mother of the Leader's wife, Ali would have great status in the clan. It was a plan that Grunn would no doubt approve, for Mara was beautiful and a hard worker. When they were younger, Mara had often talked with Seth as he sat by the stream. He knew that she did not like Nar. But that would make little difference if her mother and Grunn joined forces. Even now her mother guarded her jealously. Mara was no longer allowed to spend her time in play. Seth had noticed that whenever Mara spoke to him, Ali soon appeared and ordered her away.

"I came to warn you," Mara whispered.

Seth was so surprised to see her alone that for a minute he was speechless. "Warn me?" he managed at last.

"About the wolf."

Seth was startled. Did everyone know?

"I heard Nar and Grunn discussing it, but I already knew about the wolf. I saw you with her one day when I was searching for mushrooms. Grunn has told Nar to kill it."

"We will be careful," Esu assured her. "We are going to teach her to hunt."

"I wish I could see it," Mara said wistfully. Then she looked behind her nervously. "I'd better get back before my mother comes."

"You have another friend, it seems." Esu grinned when she had gone.

"For all the good it does me. I can't even talk to her."

"There are things worth a fight."

"How am I to fight with this leg?" Seth cried.

"Maybe there are other ways to fight. Perhaps you have the best weapon of all."

Seth looked at Esu in surprise. "What is that?"

"You are the Teller-of-Stories. What are stories anyway? Are they not good places to hide ideas?"

"Why don't you be Leader if you know so much," Seth answered crossly.

"I am not the right one. My spirits tell me to paint and to shape beautiful things."

For the next few days the boys lingered near the cave. Despite the warm weather, the hunting was still poor, and Grunn's mood was dark. He consulted Marnak often, mumbling about signs and bad spirits. Seth feared that Friend would become the scapegoat of Grunn's frustration if he discovered her presence so near to the cave. But finally he could wait no longer. Early one morning, before Nar was up, Esu and Seth took the path leading away from the clearing, doubling back when they were sure no one was following. Friend came to greet them almost immediately. She hardly hesitated now.

"You are hungry," Seth said. It was more of a statement than a question. He gave her a piece of precious meat, and she allowed him to stroke her head.

"Maybe she can't find anything to eat either," Esu said. "Or maybe she is afraid to leave her pups and hunt for food."

"She should have a pack to protect her," Seth observed. "Perhaps she is an outcast because she looks different." He reminded Esu of the packs of wild dogs that sometimes trailed after the hunters, stealing meat scraps and bones. Grunn always chased them away or killed them. "She looks a little like those dogs," he said.

"Maybe she is both," Esu suggested. Using a stick, he scratched a portrait in the dirt. "Look. Her tail is curved like a dog's, but she is colored like a wolf. Perhaps that is why she is alone. I wonder what her pups are like?"

As if remembering her motherly duties, Friend hurried away. Esu and Seth forced themselves to remain still until she had disappeared. If they stayed a distance behind, they hoped, she might not detect their scent, for the wind blew in their direction. At last they scrambled after her. Her trail twisted up the side of a mountain. The ground was rocky and steep, and Seth stumbled in spite of his walking stick.

Esu yanked him up. They could not let Friend get too far ahead—there were too many places for her to hide. Then Esu himself tripped over the knurled finger of a root and dragged Seth down with him.

"We've lost her, and it is all my fault," Esu moaned. He rubbed a skinned place on his arm.

"Maybe not," Seth said. "Listen."

They heard a tiny cry from some nearby boulders. Seth started forward, then stopped, hearing a warning growl. Esu gave him a friendly tug. "Slowly, my brother," he said. "We don't want to frighten her."

All morning they sat idle, giving Friend a chance to grow accustomed to their presence. At last, when the sun was high, they edged closer to the rocks.

"I can see her," Seth whispered happily. A few feet away, Friend lay nearly hidden at the mouth of her den. Only her eyes moved as she watched the two boys. Slowly they backed away and began to retrace their morning walk.

"Tomorrow she will be less afraid," Seth said confidently. "Eee-iii," he yelled, certain their plan was succeeding. But the yell stopped, the last note trailing to nothing, for Nar suddenly appeared on the path, glowering fiercely.

"Where have you been?" he demanded grimly.

Dog

"What do you care?" Seth asked. "You are not my leader or my father."

Esu sent Seth a warning glance. "We have been searching for bone," he said pleasantly. "I need it to make a knife."

Nar looked suspicious. "There is plenty of bone around the cave. You have been gone a long time, and yet you are empty-handed."

"I need a special kind of bone," Esu answered with a shrug. "It is not easy to find."

"You would be better to stick to your magic pictures," Nar responded heatedly. "Again and again we return from the hunt with nothing. I think the magic has left you."

"I never said my pictures were magic," Esu said. "There have been bad days before," he added reasonably.

"Marnak says your pictures are magic," Nar insisted stubbornly. A crafty look passed over his face. "Maybe you give your magic to wolves. I saw you talking with one of them. I wonder what the council would say if they knew?"

Esu sputtered indignantly. "That is stupid. Why would I do that even if I could? I have to eat, too."

"Maybe the wolves bring you food. Maybe you do this to help your friend." He paused and looked at Seth. "Perhaps you should choose your friends with care if you want to live."

"That friend saved your life."

"I did not need his help. In another minute, I would have killed the beast myself. This weakling only hoped to find favor so he could steal my rightful place as Leader of the Lion People." Nar stuck his face close to Seth's and growled, "It won't work."

Seth's jaw dropped in amazement. "I think he really believes that," he said to Esu as Nar stomped away.

"It was a mistake to save that one," Esu agreed cheerfully. "Too bad you did not have time to consider before you threw your spear." He tried to dismiss the encounter with a joke. "Shut your mouth, brother. A bee might fly in and sting you. It would be a sad day for a teller-of-stories to have a swollen tongue."

Seth chuckled, but the confrontation had upset him more than he would admit. "I think I would have had to throw the spear even if I had been given time to think," he confessed.

"I know," Esu said. "That is why I call you brother." He flung his arm around Seth's shoulders as they started back for the cave. "Listen," he said. He whistled several notes. "I've been practicing."

In spite of Nar's threats, life passed as before. The hunting was still poor, and there was some grumbling about magic. But Seth had noticed the especially dry spring weather and wondered if the game had not simply moved on in search of water. He voiced this opinion one night, and some of the men nodded, as though it was an idea they, too, had considered. Grunn, however, hooted in derision.

"One lucky throw of a spear and suddenly our Teller-of-Stories is a great hunter. Perhaps he would do better instructing the women where to find more berries."

"Aaa-eee," Seth later said to Esu. "Will I ever learn to shut my mouth? At least I didn't tell him that I had an idea about the women, too."

A slow smile spread over Esu's face. "You are full of ideas, my friend. But I think one idea at a time is too much for Grunn to manage."

Esu and Seth were still very careful about leaving the camp to see Friend and her pups, even though Nar seemed to have lost interest in their whereabouts. Friend now allowed them to romp with her pups, four wiggling balls of fur, sharp teeth, and busy tongues.

"Look at this one," Seth said. "I think it's my favorite."

"He needs a name," said Esu, laughing as the pup chased his tail, yipping fiercely.

"He looks more like a dog than the others. I think we should just call him Dog."

The pup's ears perked up as though he recognized the name. He climbed in Seth's lap and licked his face. Friend whined softly, but the pup ignored her.

"It is all right," Seth soothed. "I like your pups, but you are still my favorite."

Calmed by the gentle voice, Friend lay quietly with her head on her paws. Esu noticed, however, that her ears twitched and the hairs on her neck bristled. She whined again, softly.

"Friend seems upset today," he remarked.

"Maybe she is worried about her children. They are becoming very curious, especially Dog."

It was true that of all Friend's children, Dog was the most adventuresome. Now his little nose sniffed eagerly as he climbed around the rocks. Pausing only to nibble at a blade of grass, or growl at a crack in the boulders, he slowly edged his way out of sight. Friend, busy with the others, did not seem to notice.

"I'd better rescue him. That little fellow is going to get himself in trouble," Seth said. Esu leaned back lazily against a tree. "Go ahead. I think I will take a nap."

Seth eased down the rocks to the edge of the stream where Dog had disappeared. He walked a few more feet before he saw the pup testing the icy water. Laughing, Seth perched on a tree stump and watched. The pup stuck one paw in the water and then jerked it back, surprised. A moment later, he tried the other foot, with the same response. Then he bounced farther up the stream.

By now they were a good distance from the den. Seth sat down and dried the protesting pup on his tunic. He hugged him gently, enjoying the soft, warm smell of the puppy's fur.

A sudden scream brought him to his feet, stick and spear in hand. The puppy tumbled out of his lap and crouched a few feet away, an injured look on his face. But Seth ignored the pup in his haste to return to Esu, for he had recognized his brother's voice, though it was colored by anger and pain.

Seth knew what had happened, even before he saw the lifeless bodies of Friend and the puppies. He didn't need the evidence of the rapidly spreading pool of blood or the stricken look on Esu's face. When he reached the den and found a smirking Nar and two other young hunters, Seth felt rage wash over him, like a white heat.

"Someday you will pay for this," he shouted. He fought to keep his voice from cracking.

"I couldn't stop them," Esu cried, shaking with anger. "They were too fast."

Nar's companions looked bewildered. To them it had been a simple job of exterminating a pest. "Grunn sent us," one of them said. "We cannot have wolves stealing what little food there is."

"How did you find us?" Seth asked.

"You thought you could trick me," Nar said defiantly. "But I am a good tracker." He stood over Friend's broken body. "This fur will make a fine winter tunic."

"No," Seth screamed. He heard a soft yip from behind. Dog. He had momentarily forgotten him. It was too late for Friend, but Seth hoped he might be able to save this one pup. "Take her and leave," he commanded Nar and the others. Had they heard Dog's cry?

Nar turned to go. "Keep the dead little ones. They are not big enough for a meal," he said contemptuously. "But I would watch my step. Grunn will crush you like these wolves." He swaggered as he left, and the hunters followed obediently.

An instant later, Dog bounded into the clearing. Seth grabbed him up and held him tight, muffling his noises until he thought Nar was out of earshot. Silently he grieved.

"Grunn will kill this one, too," Esu said. "If Friend

had not trusted us, she would never have let the hunters come so near."

Seth nodded. "You are right. Friend knew something was wrong. But she depended on us to protect her. Though I failed her, I won't fail this pup."

"What can you do? He is too young to live on his own. And he will follow us back."

The afternoon passed slowly while the two boys talked over the problem. Then they heard a familiar voice. "Seth, Esu. Are you there? It is Mara."

She climbed over the rocks, turning her face away from the carnage. "I was afraid I wouldn't find you. Ohh," she said in the same breath, seeing Dog. "He is beautiful. May I touch him?"

Seth handed her the pup and stood awkwardly waiting. He knew only something important could bring Mara this far from home. Ali would surely be angry.

As though she read his thoughts, Mara gave Seth a sad smile. "Ali sent me to warn you. She is not as cruel as you may think. It is only that she is afraid, with no man to protect her. Some of the other women told her there is talk about making you Leader when you are older. I think Grunn has heard it, too. When Nar came back, bragging about killing the wolf, Grunn said you were to blame for the poor hunting. He said that you were a friend to the bad spirits, and that as long as you were alive, you would bring bad luck to the tribe. He is even telling the people that your crippled leg is a sign that you are filled with bad spirits."

"Who would believe such nonsense?" Esu asked. His voice cracked with indignation.

"There are those who speak for Seth, but right now they are outnumbered. Hunger is an enemy to reason. In time they will see the foolishness of Grunn's words, but by then it may be too late. Seth, they mean to kill you. I was bringing water from the stream when I heard Grunn talking to Nar. He told him to ambush you on the trail to the cave. Grunn said if Nar hid your body, everyone would think an animal had killed you. You must leave here before it is too late."

"Where would he go?" Esu protested. "How would he live?"

"I have been thinking about going away anyway," Seth said slowly, stunned by the day's events. "Magli said my mother's people lived somewhere beyond those mountains. Magli captured her when she was on her way to her clan's summer gathering. But if I could find them, perhaps they would let me stay."

"I'm going with you," Esu said. He held up a hand to silence Seth's protests. "I can hunt. And think of what we can do! We can see all the things the traders told us about. It will be fun."

"What of your mother and father? There is no one to miss me if I go, but you have a family," Seth countered.

"My father knows that my feet itch to see more than this valley. He will understand. An itch that cannot be scratched is a terrible thing."

Mara smiled. "Ali asked your father for advice, Esu.

He does know you. He has sent your robes and weapons, and your mother even packed some food."

"Then it is settled. Tell them we shall return when we have seen all the world and learned what we can."

"I owe you my life," Seth said to Mara. "I will not forget."

Reluctantly Mara handed back the pup. Then she touched Seth's face gently. "I must return before Grunn suspects." Her eyes were sad. "Come back someday." She stepped away and then stopped once more. "You are wrong about one thing. Someone will miss you."

"Who?"

"I will miss you," she answered softly. An instant later, she had disappeared from view.

Seth and Esu worked quickly, dividing up the supplies. Esu moved cheerfully, as though leaving on a day's adventure, but Seth was pensive, unsure he was doing the right thing. He thought back on his life with the Lion People. His stories had been the threads that connected all their lives. But good or bad, weak or strong, the Lion People were bound together in a way no story could explain. Although he had told himself his tribespeople meant nothing to him, now that it was time to leave he understood his ties to them. Kindly Jon-tu and his wife, sour-faced Ali who had saved his life, wrinkled Marnak and his knowledge of magic, Mara, and all the others were a part of himself. Now the Lion People would have two less to make them great.

"Come on," Esu urged. "We need to get far enough

away that our camp will not be seen tonight."

Seth turned, trying to catch one last glimpse of home. But the cave was hidden by the rocks. There was a thickness in his throat that made it difficult to swallow. He held up his fist in a silent vow. "Someday, I will see the Lion People again."

Alone

Seth lifted Dog from his pack and put him down for a romp. "Now, don't get any ideas about jumping in the river," he warned. "You're getting too big for me to rescue."

In the weeks since the boys' journey had begun, Dog had grown at an alarming rate. From a small ball of fluff, he had become almost too heavy for Seth to carry.

Happy to be free, Dog yipped and chased his tail.

Around and around he wound himself until he finally fell over in a heap. Seth laughed. "What would your mother think of your acting so foolish?" Remembering Friend, Seth felt a sudden stab of pain, and he busied himself making camp to clear his mind.

At Esu's suggestion, they had followed the stream. "That way we will always have water," he had reasoned. "And I can hunt animals who come to drink."

It had been a good plan. After tumbling down the hills where the Lion People made their home, the stream gradually widened as it passed through the valley. In the hills the stream had been clear and cool, but on the flat land it had become a muddy brown river. Still, the walking was easier, except for places where they had to push through tall grasses and brush. Already they were far away from the cave. Looking back, Seth could see the nearby hills and the taller peaks beyond. From the cave the peaks seemed impossibly tall and forbidding, but from this distance they seemed small and unimportant.

On the first day the boys had walked together all day, then they had fallen into a daily routine. Toward afternoon, Esu would scout ahead, looking for the evening meal, while Seth stayed behind to make camp. Esu was not the best hunter, Seth had discovered. Many times he became so interested in exploring that dinner was forgotten. But Seth soon adjusted to his friend's wild enthusiasm, and it was hard to be disappointed at the lack of meat for supper when Esu described some wondrous thing he'd found. At times like this, his eyes sparkled and he tugged at his curly hair as he talked. Seth learned how to fill in the gaps in the meals by digging up roots and searching the woods for berries. Now he was grateful for the time he had spent watching the women doing the same work.

Soon after Esu had left that afternoon, Seth had found a source of honey by following some bees to a decaying old tree not far from the river.

He whistled for Dog. Seth was trying to teach the pup to come with that signal, and already he seemed to understand it, even if he didn't always respond. This time he did, bounding out of the brush, wagging his tail eagerly.

"Today we are going to have something special," he told Dog. "And you will be safer here." He took a length of leather and tied the dog to a tree. "It is for your own good," he said firmly, chuckling at the pup's sad face.

Smiling at the thought of the sticky treat, he set to work piling dried grass on the ground beneath the entrance to the hive. Magli had taught him how to steal the honey without getting stung. Moving quietly, so not to disturb the bees, Seth took his fire rocks from the pouch around his neck. He struck the iron pyrite and flint several times before a small flame curled upward from the grass. Then quickly he added twigs and threw in some damp leaves and green wood to produce good thick smoke.

Resting against a tree, Seth waited for the smoke to make the bees sluggish and confused. He did not have to wait long. Then, holding his breath, he groped blindly for the honeycomb. As soon as his fingers closed in over the sticky goodness, he lifted it out, still dripping, and placed it in a wooden bowl. This portion he would share with Esu, but the honey on his fingers he licked slowly, savoring the taste to make it last.

Catching sight of Dog's woebegone expression, he dipped his fingers into the bowl and allowed the pup to lick his hands. Dog's warm pink tongue tickled, and Seth smiled.

Then, remembering his friend, Seth glanced at the sky. Esu would be returning soon. Seth worked quickly, first saving some burning sticks for their evening fire, and finally extinguishing the flames under the bee tree with water. This done, he untied Dog and leaned back against some rocks to wait for Esu's return. The afternoon was warm, however, and it wasn't long before he drifted off.

"Yee, yee, yee." Dog's squeals interrupted his daydreams. The pup ran to Seth, batting at his nose.

"A fine hunter you are." Seth laughed. "We have already stolen their honey. Did you think the bees would be happy to see you?" He carried Dog to the riverbank and scooped up soft mud to soothe his nose. In a few minutes, Dog had stopped trembling and was restored to his wiggling good humor.

"How could anyone think you would bring bad magic?" Seth asked as he stroked the pup.

"Meat tonight," Esu announced, bursting into the clearing. He held up a fine fat rabbit. It was soon skinned and threaded on a stick over the fire that Seth had built. The boys' mouths watered, and they sampled the honey while they watched their meal cook.

"I am worried about the mountains up ahead," Esu said. "They are higher than we thought. I am afraid the climb will be difficult with your bad leg."

"I will make it," Seth said proudly. Although the mountains seemed formidable as they came closer, Seth had felt his body growing stronger every day. He even looked stronger. His arms were tanned, and he noticed a faint stubble on his chin, brown like his hair. Esu's face, on the other hand, was still smooth, although his fair skin meant he usually had a peeling sunburn across his nose.

Seth's confidence in his new strength did not convince Esu. "I don't know if we can make it," he said, "unless I find a passageway. While you stay here with Dog, I'll go ahead and scout. The trip should only take me three days."

Unhappily Seth agreed. Together they could face many enemies, but apart, a lot could happen. He knew Esu was right, however. Even though it was barely summer, it would take them weeks to cross the mountains, and winter would come early in the higher peaks.

"Maybe we should not go over the mountains. We could try another direction instead," he suggested.

"The traders travel across the mountains. That is why I am sure there is a passage," Esu replied.

Seth sighed. Once his friend's mind was made up, there was no changing it. And perhaps if they did reach the other side, they would find his mother's people. Curiously, he found himself longing for home, and each step away made it more doubtful he would ever return. Now it seemed that life had been so much easier when all he had to do was listen to Nar's taunts. Here there were decisions to be made every day. Esu, on the other hand, seemed not to miss the Lion People at all. Seth was beginning to suspect that Esu would always be eager to scale the next mountain.

When Esu left the next morning, Seth felt a moment of emptiness that made him hug Dog so close the pup wiggled to escape. He watched Esu run lightly along the riverbank, pausing once to hold up his hand in farewell, until he was only a tiny dot in the distance. At least he had Dog, Seth thought. There were signs now of the magnificent beast Dog would become, and Seth felt proud to have won his love.

Dog settled down for a nap as Seth gathered wood and made his camp as comfortable as possible. The three days loomed endlessly ahead. Seth spent the rest of the morning exploring the nearby woods and searching for food. That evening he shared with Dog the small bit of rabbit he'd saved from the night before, and finished the last of the honey.

The next morning, Seth felt more cheerful. He only had to make it through this day, for tomorrow Esu would return. Perhaps, he thought, he could try to catch a few fish from the river to fill up his time.

He kicked dirt and grass over the remains of last night's fire and set off for the riverbank. It was there that he spotted the six men. Even from some distance away, they were fierce-looking, and Seth's heart beat wildly as he tried to decide what to do. If they were friendly, they might know an easy way over the mountains. If not, he could be captured or even killed. Staying concealed seemed the wisest move.

Stuffing his pack and sleeping skin behind some rocks, he dove into a thicket. The vines scratched and tore at his skin, but they provided good cover. The men would pass quite close to this hiding place. Seth patted Dog, willing him to be silent, and firmly gripped his spear. It would be a useless weapon against so many, he knew. Even so, he felt better holding it. Now he wished his walking stick really did contain magic. His stick! In his haste, he had forgotten it. It lay in plain sight only a few feet away, and it was too late to try and retrieve it.

It was clear the men had been hunting. They had a quartered deer among them, and one man struggled to carry the antlers, which were nearly as wide as Seth was tall. Although some of their words sounded oddly familiar, they spoke a strange language. The leader was a dark, swarthy man, taller than the others. His face was heavily bearded, nearly hiding his features. Seth watched him point into the woods, perhaps suggesting a shortcut. While the other men hesitated, the two carrying the body of the deer shifted the weight uncomfortably. Then everyone nodded in agreement. A moment later they were gone.

Seth waited a long while before he crawled out of the thicket and took up his stick. That night he didn't make a fire, fearful that the fierce strangers lived somewhere nearby. Miserable, he huddled in his skins and chewed on a few berries. A light rain began, and a thunderstorm streaked the nearby hills. Seth wondered if Esu had found a safe shelter for the night.

It rained all night, and the next morning the river was swollen and its banks were slippery with mud. Seth climbed some rocks high enough for a long-distance view. The forest swept empty and silent to the edge of the mountains. He tried not to worry. It was still early, he thought, and perhaps the rain had delayed Esu's return.

By midday the sky was sullen and dark, and the air was sticky and oppressively hot. At home on a day like this, Seth would have remained in the cave, taking comfort in its coolness. Here there was no relief from the heat, and mosquitoes nibbled at his arms and face. He had never felt so miserable and alone.

It was evening before Seth admitted to himself that Esu would not return that day. He fought the idea of Esu's encountering the hunters. But there was an acid taste in his mouth, and he was nervous, jumping at the slightest sound.

Dog seemed to sense his mood and whined softly. Seth considered a fire. He had not seen any sign of the men or a village from his lookout up on the rocks. At last he decided it was worth the risk. Besides, without a fire, Esu might have difficulty finding him if he came back during the night. He curled up with Dog close to the flames and tried unsuccessfully to sleep. At dawn there was still no sign of his friend.

With Dog at his heels, Seth climbed the rocks for one last look for Esu. He almost convinced himself he would see him running to the clearing, laughing and full of excuses for his late return. But, straining his eyes in every direction, Seth saw no one. It was as though he were alone in the world.

"Stay close to me," he told Dog sternly. "I need you."

Heedless, Dog bounded eagerly after a rabbit. He crashed through the woods, too young to really hunt, yipping and enjoying the run.

Seth felt a moment of panic, but he shrugged it off. If the men had not been close enough to see the fire, they surely would not be close enough to hear a noisy pup. "You make more racket than a herd of bison," Seth scolded when Dog returned a short time later. Only briefly did Dog look ashamed before his usual high spirits took over and he covered Seth with wet licks.

"You need a mother to show you how to hunt," Seth said, laughing. "I am afraid I will not make a good teacher." He sat, unmindful of the mud, rubbing Dog's ears. "I wish you and I could talk," he added. "You could help me decide what we will do if Esu doesn't return."

By noon the storm had rolled back, this time wild and threatening. Thunder rumbled and cracked, and rain fell in sheets. Dog shivered violently at every lightning strike. The squall lasted all afternoon and into the night. All along the river, the land was too flat to offer any protection. Seth was forced to huddle under his skins, lonely, wet, and cold, with only a frightened Dog for company.

Captured!

Morning brought cooler weather and an end to the rain. Seth shivered as he struggled to start a fire with the wet kindling. Finally he gave up and started walking toward the mountains to look for some sign of Esu. By afternoon he was forced to admit defeat. Whatever signs there might have been had been washed away by the rain and mud. The thought of Esu dead or seriously hurt filled him with a numbing sadness, and it was hard for Seth to think clearly. Yet he knew he must plan carefully if he wanted to survive. Again and again, his thoughts returned to the fierce men he had seen on the trail. Surely they were the reason he hadn't found Esu. What if they had captured him? Even as Seth worried, his friend might be a slave to the harsh-looking strangers. Or maybe Esu had met them, and they had pointed out a route. Maybe he had waited out the storm with them. At least these possibilities gave Seth hope.

"Esu was wrong. I wouldn't be a good leader at all. This is my first real problem, and I don't know what to do," Seth said out loud. Cupping his chin in his hands, he sat glumly, weighing his choices. Dog stayed patiently by his side as though he understood his master's distress.

"We'll go back and look for the hunters," Seth said at last. "So many men should have left signs we can follow even with the rain." Making this decision cheered him a little. At least now he and Dog would not be simply waiting.

He waited until the next morning, however, to head into the forest. By then the sun had dried the ground enough to make walking a little easier. From where Seth had spotted them, the men had veered away from the river toward the foothills. He knew the hunters would not have carried the deer they killed for more than a day. With a little good fortune, Seth thought, he would find their home in one of the valleys near the mountains.

Even to his inexperienced eyes, the trail was easy to follow. The men had not been careful as they walked, and there were enough broken limbs and smashed plants to mark their route clearly.

For most of that day, Dog trotted willingly at Seth's side, with only a few brief side trips of his own. Toward evening, however, the pup disappeared for so long that Seth became worried. But when he whistled, Dog returned almost instantly, and Seth was amazed to see a good-size rabbit in his jaws.

In his astonishment, Seth gave a whoop. "Aaa-eee. We were right after all. You can be taught to hunt." Then he froze for a moment, silently berating himself for his stupidity. He would not last very long alone if he could not control his exuberance better than that. This time, though, luck was with him and the woods remained silent.

He bent down to quietly coax Dog into sharing his meal. Briefly he wondered how Dog had managed to snare the rabbit, but he didn't ponder the question for long. His mouth was already watering. Quickly he built a fire, hoping the forest would conceal the smoke.

When the rabbit was ready to eat, Seth gave a portion to Dog. "It is much better cooked, don't you agree?" Seth asked him. Dog gobbled his share and begged for more, but as before, Seth saved some for morning. "We will spend the night here," Seth said when they had finished the meal. "I don't think the hunters' home can be far now." He wondered what he would do when he found it. Shrugging, he prepared for sleep. He would think about that when the time came.

Exhaustion conquered Seth's fears and brought deep, restful sleep. After a hasty breakfast the following morning, he set off again. Almost immediately he saw that he was near his destination: well-worn paths, cut trees and brush, and, most convincingly, the smell of wood fires and cooking meat. Dog smelled it, too, and Seth had to tuck the pup back in the pack to keep him from running ahead.

At last, leaving the forest cover, he came to a broad outcropping of rocks. On a ledge overlooking a wide green valley, he heard the sound of children at play and, curiously, the barking of dogs. Still holding Dog, Seth peered over the ridge.

He gasped in amazement. Never had he seen so many people in one place, many times more than the Lion People. On a cleared patch of land, there were dwellings of mud and stone clustered close together. A small enclosure of logs, stone, and thorn bushes held sheep and goats. Men and women were both tending a large field of grain. The children were playing near the huts, many of them romping with lean brown dogs. Some of these same creatures napped in perfect ease in the shade of the houses. There were none of them as beautiful as Dog, but it was plain to Seth that he was not the first to make friends with such animals.

A woman emerged from one of the huts, carrying a clay jar for water. Even from this distance, Seth could see it was far finer than the dried-mud and reed pots made by his own people. She waved a greeting to the men tending a fire in a huge pit, which was surrounded by a great many jars and pots.

Seth was so absorbed by the wealth of new sights that he lost track of Dog. To his dismay he saw him streaking gleefully down the ledge toward the town. Seth whistled their signal, but dog was long past hearing and too happy at seeing his own kind. He yipped excitedly, ears and tail flying in the wind. Seth watched a scruffy-looking male walk toward Dog. From his menacing pose, Seth knew the dog did not welcome the noisy newcomer, but Dog was too eager to notice.

Distracted by Dog's dangerous situation, Seth did not realize his own life was in greater danger until it was too late. He sensed, rather than heard, something behind him and twisted around to see three men approaching stealthily. Each held a strange weapon, consisting of a curved piece and a small but deadly-looking spear. Seth used his walking stick to push himself up and face the trio.

One of them spoke. He was tall, young, and light-haired, and, except for a scowl, his face might have been considered pleasant. He wore a necklace of curved teeth, and his tunic was decorated with a beaded hawk. Seth fought the urge to reach out his hand. It was the most beautiful beading he had ever seen.

Seth could not grasp the meaning of the man's strange words, and yet again he felt there was something familiar about them. The language was not too different from his own. He shrugged to show he did not understand, and the men talked for a minute among themselves.

Then one of them noticed Seth's walking stick. He grabbed it so suddenly that Seth would have fallen if Hawk Shirt hadn't unexpectedly reached out to steady him. He spoke sharply to the man with the stick and pointed to Seth's leg. A bit sheepishly, the man handed back the stick. Clearly, he had thought it was a weapon of some sort. Hawk Shirt smiled and pointed to the carved deer. Perhaps, Seth thought, he thinks I'm the artist.

Seth shook his head. "My friend Esu made it." The men did not seem to recognize the name. They conferred among themselves again as though they did not know quite what to do next.

Dog picked that moment to return. His tail was tucked between his legs and one ear was torn a little. But seeing his master restored him instantly to good spirits. He wiggled happily and licked Seth. At the sight of Dog, the men seemed to relax, and they chuckled. When they motioned for Seth to go with them to the village, their faces no longer looked unfriendly, and they carried their weapons down.

Still, Seth found it hard to look brave. As they approached the village, men, women, and children gathered around him, chattering, reaching out to touch his clothes and his stick. Hawk Shirt did not pause. He pushed his way good-naturedly through the crowd until they reached one of the huts. Then, stooping to enter, he waved at Seth to follow.

The hut was as plain inside as out. But it was roomier than Seth had expected, and clean. Sleeping skins and mats were rolled to one side under some small wooden benches. There were several pots similar to the ones he had observed from the ledge, and up close he could see they were festooned with an intricate design. A smell came from one of them that made his mouth water with hunger.

In one corner of the hut sat a woman, quietly braiding some beads in her hair. When Seth entered, she looked up in surprise. But after Hawk Shirt spoke to her, she smiled and gave Seth a bowl of the pungent stew, a goat meat and vegetable mixture.

Seth gulped down the thick stew, his first real meal since the rabbit. In spite of his hunger, he dug out several pieces of meat for Dog, and the woman filled his bowl again. Secretly he watched her while he ate, amazed by her dress. Except for the beads, Hawk Shirt dressed very much like a man of the Lion People. But the woman wore a long dress of a material Seth had never seen. It was soft and creamy ivory-colored, and like the man's shirt it was beautifully beaded. On her arms were two bands of ivory.

Hawk Shirt waited until Seth had finished eating. Then he sat down and studied Seth intently. Pointing to himself, he said, "Abed." Pointing to the woman, he said, "Sari."

The message was clear. Seth tapped his chest. "Seth."

Then, using sign language, he tried to ask about Esu, but he could not make himself understood. Suddenly Sari pointed to the deer carved on Seth's walking stick and said something in an excited voice. From under one of the robes she brought out a knife, carved with the same running deer.

"That's Esu's. I was right. He is here."

Once again Abed led him through the crowds of curious onlookers. Seth's stomach churned with dread. He knew the knife was Esu's most prized possession. He would never willingly part with it.

Seth followed Abed past several huts crowded together like a wasps' nest. Finally he stopped in front of one that was slightly set apart from the others. Fearing what he would find, Seth entered.

New Friends

"Esu," he gasped, sure for a moment his friend was dead. Then, as his eyes adjusted to the dim light, Seth saw a small movement of breath. Esu was pale, and there was a deep gash on his head. He had been placed on a mat of woven reeds, and around his body a leering row of skulls kept watch with empty eyes. An old man, wizened and nearly hairless, chanted as he rocked slowly back and forth. At Seth's arrival, he looked up and grinned, showing a mouth nearly empty of teeth. Abed watched politely as Seth knelt on the dirt floor beside his friend, and the old man resumed his chanting as though he had forgotten the visitor.

Seth's thoughts whirled. The old man was obviously some kind of magic keeper or healer. But what had happened to Esu? The people had seemed friendly. Had they done this?

Esu's head turned slightly. "Esu, I am here," Seth said.

At first Esu did not seem to remember him. Then his eyes cleared and he spoke so weakly that Seth had to put his head close to hear.

"Fell. Rocks were slippery after the rain."

Seth sighed with relief. So these people who kept goats had saved Esu after all. When Esu's eyes closed again and he appeared to be sleeping, Seth drew his knees under his chin and watched the healer at work. Abed urged him to leave the hut, but Seth shook his head stubbornly. Now that he had found his brother, he was determined not to leave until he knew he would live. Nodding to show he understood, Abed spoke quietly to the old man and then left the hut. The healer ignored Seth as he chanted and rocked. At last the soothing rhythm lulled Seth himself into a troubled, dream-filled sleep that lasted until morning.

He awoke with a guilty start. His brother might be dying, and he could not even stay awake. But a quick glance at Esu made him feel better. Although still sleeping, he did not look quite as pale. The old man gave Seth a smile and a satisfied nod.

When Abed appeared, Seth gratefully followed him back to his hut. While he ate his morning meal, Seth decided he liked the wrinkled old man caring for Esu. He would trust him. He had no choice really, but he felt better knowing he was in the old healer's care.

That morning Seth learned that Abed, the headman, and Sari, his wife, were the leaders of the Goat People. Abed was the exact opposite of Grunn. A strong and clever leader, he was also friendly and kind. Everyone seemed to love him, from the oldest man to the youngest child. In fact, the children followed him as he went about his business. Crowding around him, they would shout, "A bear, Abed. Be a bear."

Then Abed, good-naturedly as always, covered himself with a thick bear robe and chased them, growling so fiercely the children dissolved into giggles. At the sight of the big man romping with the children, Seth smiled.

"That is how a leader should be," he told Esu the following morning. Esu was sitting up, still weak, but his eyes burned with their familiar curiosity.

"Do you know how many things we can learn here?" he asked. "Look at those pots, and the small spears. We should stay for a while before we go on with our journey."

"Don't you miss your mother and father?"

"Sometimes," Esu admitted. "But there are too many places to see first. By the time I am well, it will be too late to cross the mountains. We can go in the spring."

Seth nodded. How could he refuse? This was Esu,

his brother, and he owed him so much. Without Esu, he might still be at the cave, suffering the insults of Nar and his friends, or even dead.

While Esu healed, Seth spent most of his time with Domo, the herder, and the goats. Even with his crippled leg, Seth could help, and more than that, he found that he enjoyed the shaggy, horned beasts. Domo taught him how to protect the herd, keeping a sharp eye open for predators. Dog enjoyed the watch also, often leaping up to drive back a straggler. Seth noticed Domo studying the half-wild dogs in the camp, and he knew he was wondering if they, too, could be trained like Dog.

By the time Artu, the healer, allowed Esu to leave his bed, Seth had learned a few words of the Goat People's language. With the help of signs, he could converse with his new friends.

Proudly Seth took Esu around the village, showing him everything. Esu was bored with the animals, but he was interested in the fiery pit. "They make the pots out of a special river clay," he told Seth. "And when they bake them in the pit, the pots become as hard as stone."

Esu recovered his strength quickly, and the two boys settled into the life of the village. With Abed's help, Esu and Seth made the small spears and bows used by the Goat People. After much practice, the two boys became nearly as skilled with the weapon as were the other men. Still, they were more comfortable with their own spears, and it was Esu's that brought down an attacking lion one night, making him a hero.

It was an old lion, or perhaps it never would have ventured so close to the village. Stealthily it stalked a group of children playing away from the huts in the shade of some trees. Esu saw it as he made his way home from the pit. He had just learned a new trick, he told Seth later. One of the men had heated bone enough to make it bend. Esu was dreaming of all the things he could make with this new knowledge when his thoughts were interrupted by a woman's screams. Without hesitation, Esu's spear sailed through the air and found its mark.

"There wasn't time to think of danger," Esu stated modestly. "I just threw."

"That's what happened when I saved Nar," Seth replied, chuckling. "But this lion skin is a much nicer prize than Nar."

"Abed told me he wants us to stay," Esu said, turning serious. "He wants to have a feast and make us one of the Goat People."

"How did you answer?"

Esu looked surprised. "I said that we were honored, but that we were leaving as soon as we could get over the mountains."

Seth tried to hide his disappointment. "I will have to make a new story for your lion kill."

"You will have to add some interesting things, or it won't be much of a story."

"Maybe it is always that way. Perhaps if men had

time to think, they would not be so brave."

"There is a different kind of bravery. You have it, brother, fighting your leg, doing what other men do," Esu said.

Seth felt his face grow hot. "I didn't until you made the stick and helped me."

Esu grinned. "You were brave. You just needed me to remind you."

Even after he was well, Esu continued to live with Artu. He had grown fond of the old man during the long days while he waited for his body to heal. But Seth stayed in the house of Abed and Sari. The language of the Goat People became easier for him as time went by, and he practiced by telling them stories of the Lion People.

One day he recalled how Magli had captured a bride, bringing her home to become his mother. Sari leaned forward, listening intently.

"You say your mother was on her way to a summer clan meeting when she was taken?"

"That is what Magli said," Seth said, nodding.

Sari gave Abed a strange look. "My oldest sister disappeared many years ago. She was on her way to a summer clan meeting, too. We thought she was dead. She was called Nani."

The hut was quiet while Seth digested this information. "That was my mother's name. But she lived near a land of thundering water. My father said she often told him about it."

Abed nodded. "It is not far from here. We do not go there often, though, because there are many lions nearby."

"You are my family," Sari said at last.

Wonderingly Seth looked at his mother's sister. His mother had never seemed quite real, a shadowy memory recalled mainly through Magli's stories. Now she was a person. If she was as pretty as Sari, it was no wonder Magli had loved her. And to find that he had a family. Aaa-eee, it made his heart sing. If only he could stay here with his mother's people. Already he had thought of some ideas he would like to try. What if they built the fence out of trees instead of brush? Maybe they could dig a path from the river to bring water to the far end of the grainfield. The Goat People listened to his ideas with interest instead of the dark suspicion he faced from Grunn.

As if he had read Seth's mind, Abed spoke. "I have thought long on a certain matter. This valley is a good place. The earth grows more grain than we need, and there is enough water and meat. You said the hunting was no longer good where the Lion People live. We were friends, and now it seems we are kin. If your people would come, we could teach them how to build houses and keep goats. We could live together, as family."

"Grunn would never agree," Seth said. "But it would be a good thing."

"If you ever go back, you can tell them that Abed and the Goat People would welcome them as friends."

Abed stood up. "You are a teller-of-stories. You should talk to Grandmother, the keeper of our stories. This is something that should be remembered, that the Lion People and the Goat People are joined by their son Seth."

"Your teller-of-stories is a woman?" Seth found this hard to believe, though he knew that the women and men were nearly equal among the Goat People. Many times he had heard Abed ask Sari's advice. He laughed, imagining Grunn seeking a woman's opinion. To him it would have been an insult to have a woman admitted to the fire circle.

Without answering Seth's question, Abed was already striding out of the hut. Seth hurried to keep up with the man's usual long-legged pace. Finally Abed stopped and poked his head inside one of the huts. "Grandmother. Are you here? There is someone to see you."

"I am waiting," said a soft voice. Stepping through the doorway, Seth saw an old woman seated on a mat. She was bent with age, but her eyes were clear and sparkled like a young girl's. Seth liked her instantly, though he was speechless after Abed introduced him and left. Grandmother stared intently, as though measuring Seth's worth.

"I was wondering when you would come."

"How could you know I would come?"

"It is nothing strange," she said, chuckling. "My bones are too old to leave my hut. But others come here. They tell me things. Many are surprised to see a teller-of-stories who is so young."

"I am surprised to see a teller-of-stories who is a woman," Seth blurted, without thinking.

Grandmother chuckled merrily. "Then we start even. Each of us surprised at the other."

He told her about Magli and Grunn. He told her about Dog and how they had been forced to leave. Through it all she listened quietly, nodding now and then.

"You have had many adventures for one so young." Reaching out, she stroked Dog, who had followed Seth into the hut.

"The wolf stays with its pack and avoids man. That is its nature. The dog comes to scavenge at our fire. That is its nature. But this one is like neither. He stays with you because of love. I see it in his eyes. Perhaps he is both wolf and dog." She was silent for a time. Then she looked at Seth. "I am curious about you. Are you a wolf or a dog?"

"What do you mean?" Seth stammered.

"Your friend is like the dog. He goes free wherever there are scraps to find. That is good, for that is his nature. But I think you are like the wolf, longing for your family."

"Esu wants to go on," Seth said dully. "Yet he is more than a friend. He is a brother. He did not have to come with me, but he did."

"A brother is a wonderful thing. Yet you are not

free like him. His heart is like the bird, flying from place to place, always searching for one more thing to love. You are the Teller-of-Stories. It is not a gift to be taken lightly. You hold the past for your people in your heart. And maybe, with the new skills you have learned, you also hold their future. You must weigh these things before you decide."

"Even if I go back, they may not listen."

"They may not. Perhaps you will have to show them. Maybe you will have more power as the Teller-of-Stories than any leader."

"I owe Esu too much to leave him," he sighed.

"That is something you will have to decide for yourself." The old woman smiled suddenly. "You are very young. It may be that the time has not come for you to return to your people."

After he left Grandmother's hut, Seth searched for Esu. He found him at last near the fire pit, crafting the bent bone. Seth told Esu about Grandmother, though not about their curious conversation. "Once I did not belong anywhere," he said. "Now I have two homes."

"And you will have many more," Esu added, returning to his work.

Seth wandered to a nearby stream and stared at his image. Why were things so simple for Esu? Seth's own reflection showed someone who was nearly a man. He had grown taller, and though his leg was still crippled, he looked stronger. Yet inside, he was afraid. He buried his face in Dog's fur and sobbed, "Tell me what to do, Dog. Tell me what to do."

"It will be hard to leave the Goat People," he said to Esu one day in early spring. Seth had found his brother a little way from the village, gazing at the mountains with a hungry look. Dog sat beside them as they talked. His coat had grown thick over the mild winter, and now when he scratched, great billows of hair shook loose.

"I like it here, too," Esu admitted. "But there is a very pretty sister of Abed who is making me nervous. She peeks at me and giggles. Next she will have me working in the fields, trapped here forever."

"Would that be so terrible?" Seth asked. The image of Mara went through his mind.

"How can you ask such a question? Did you hear those traders who came not long ago? They go to a city, a place much more wonderful than this. So many people you could not find a number to count them. And houses. Not like these poor huts, but with many rooms and some with steps that go up. Imagine! A house on top of a house. We must see that. The snow is nearly gone from the mountains. I think it is time to go."

"I am ready," Seth answered flatly.

Their new friends greeted the news of their departure with tears and presents. When they left, their packs were filled with gifts. From Sari there were new tunics and pants of the softest leather, with beaded designs. Her eyes looked sad when she hugged him. "My sister would have been happy to see what a fine son she had," she said.

From the mothers of the children Esu had saved there were warm leather shoes, strips of dried meat and fruit, and an extra tunic made from a plant they called flax.

Abed gave them new bows and a supply of the little spears. Even Artu gave them a gift. "It is an amulet to give you good magic," he said, hanging the small pouches around their necks. Tears streamed down his leathery cheeks.

The only one missing was Grandmother. Seth searched through the crowd, hoping to see her, but she was not there.

Esu looked jaunty in his new clothes. Surrounded by several girls from the village, he said, "Maybe I will come back someday." But his eyes were turned to the mountains.

At the top of the hill, Seth stopped for one last look. He could see Abed, romping in a game of bear with the children. Domo was with his goats. Then he saw Grandmother standing beside her house. She seemed to be staring at him, although Seth knew that she could not see him at that distance. Dog barked, urging him to hurry on.

"I'm coming," he called. When he looked back at Grandmother's house, the old woman was no longer there.

The Decision

For the next few days, Esu filled the time talking of dreams and plans. "In the city, the people keep the skulls of their ancestors in their homes. On a little bench," he said.

"Why would they do that?" Seth asked, trying to conceal his restlessness.

"How would I know?" Esu shrugged. "I only know what the traders told me. Maybe that is the way they do their magic."

Seth shuddered. "I think I like Artu's magic better." He rubbed the tiny pouch around his neck.

"Don't worry, my brother. I will see that your head stays attached to the rest of you. I do not think I would sleep with your skull watching over me.

"There are many people who make things of great beauty in the city," Esu went on seriously. "Perhaps one of them would teach me his secrets."

"You already make things of great beauty," Seth said. "Like my stick. What could be better?"

Esu grinned and reached into his pouch. "I have been practicing." He handed Seth a tiny figure.

Seth studied the delicate carving. It was a lion, but its head was a man. "It is Abed," he exclaimed.

"When I look at someone, I think of an animal. Grunn, for instance, makes me think of a bison."

Seth grinned. "I have thought that, too. What am I?"

"You are a wolf. Strong and true, and you yearn for a family."

"I think you are a deer, running through the forest, never stopping."

"A wolf, and a deer, and a dog. Strange traveling companions, wouldn't you say?" Before Seth could answer, he held up his hand. Two long-legged water birds stood in the reeds along the wide and muddy river. Esu's bow sliced through the air. Dog was off in a flash, wading through the brown water. He brought the bird back and laid it at Seth's feet.

"He always takes them to you," Esu grumbled good-naturedly. "Maybe he thinks you are a better cook."

They decided then to make camp for the night, and while Esu gathered wood for the fire, Seth prepared the bird. He cleaned it and laced it on a stick, which he balanced on two forked pieces on each side of the fire. Finally he sprinkled the bird with a few grains of their precious salt, a gift from Abed. When the fire died down to coals, Seth searched the area for something to go with the meat. It did not take long to find some wild onions, and, in a nearby bog, a rare treat—blueberries!

When he returned to camp, Esu was swimming in the river. "My stomach was getting impatient, watching the meat cook," he explained.

Pulling off his leggings, Seth joined him in the water. Despite his leg, he was, if anything, a better swimmer than Esu.

Swimming was something new to both boys. There had been little chance to learn in the shallow stream near the cave. But Abed's people swam at a lake close to the town, and both boys had learned quickly.

"Let's go see if that bird is finally done," Esu suggested, shivering. "I am hungry enough to eat two birds."

They swam back to their camp. To their astonishment, they discovered they were not alone. Crowded around the campfire were thirteen strange people. They looked dusty and tired, and their clothes were little more than crude skins. The men jabbered excitedly and gestured at the bird, roasted now to a golden brown.

"What should we do?" Seth whispered.

"I think they are friendly," Esu said, tugging on his leggings. "They have women and a child with them. But there goes our dinner. They look hungry."

Through gestures, the leader of this ragged band of nomads explained that they needed a place to stop while one of the women gave birth. Politely they offered to add what they had to the feast of roasted bird and berries. It was mostly frogs and grubs and a few wild carrots and nuts.

After Esu gave them some salt, one of the women pushed forward a scrawny bare-bottomed child, just barely able to walk. The woman pointed to Esu and then to the child.

The boys understood. So few babies survived this meager existence that the children were not even named until they were a year old. For the gift of salt, the woman would give her child Esu's name. Impulsively Seth handed the child the lion carving. He meant it for a toy. The mother looked pleased.

In the morning the people had gone, as quietly as they had come. "I wonder if they thought your carving was some kind of magic," Seth said.

"They could use a little magic," Esu said.

Seth thought of the Lion People. Did the traders who visited them feel the same pity for his people that he had felt for the nomads? And if the hunting did not improve, would the Lion People be forced again into wandering, always searching for food? Suddenly Seth's mind was made up. He knew what he must do. He at least owed his people the knowledge that they had a choice. He would return and recount what he had seen. If he told his stories skillfully, perhaps they would listen, even Grunn.

He turned to Esu, determined but remorseful. "I have to go back."

"You can't mean that," Esu said. "What about all our plans?"

"Your plans, not mine. I have to help them."

"Grunn will never let you come back."

"I have to take that chance. You were the one who was always telling me what a good leader I could be. But having great ideas isn't enough. A good leader has to take responsibility for those ideas. All my life I've felt sorry for myself because no one listened to me. My leg was my excuse, but it wasn't that. I was never willing to stand up for what I believed." Seth paused. "Come with me. I need a friend. Maybe later we can travel to the city."

Esu scowled. "I came with you, took care of you. What about me? Am I not your brother?"

"You are my brother. But I must do this. Please come with me."

Stubbornly Esu shook his head. "I have traveled all this way. I will not go back until I have seen, with my own eyes, what I've dreamed about." Esu grabbed Seth's shoulders and shook him slightly. "You are only a boy. Wait awhile. There is still much to discover. And how will you make it alone? You will get lost, or a wild animal will eat you."

Seth shrugged. "I am going back."

"I am not ready," Esu shouted.

"I am."

Without another word, Esu picked up his pack and walked away.

"Don't be angry, my brother," Seth called after him. But Esu did not stop. Seth stood and watched him with misty eyes until he was no more than a tiny speck.

The Thundering Water

Without Esu's company, Seth's days were empty and bleak. Had it not been for Dog, always at his side, Seth thought he might have died of loneliness. The first two days alone, he looked behind him often, sure he would see Esu waving hello, their argument forgotten. But soon he gave up and concentrated on the journey home. He kept up a punishing pace, pausing only long enough to scavenge for food and sleep restlessly through the darkest hours of the night.

He knew the general direction to the cave of the Lion People, but he had not been trained by the hunters with the other boys in the tribe. By watching the rising and setting sun, Seth followed what he hoped was a straighter route home than the journey out. It would not take him back to the Goat People, but he thought that was wise. If he returned to their village, they might weaken his resolve and tempt him to stay.

Early on the sixth day, he found his way was blocked by a river. This was not the same one he had followed with Esu. That river had been smooth, and muddy, meandering peacefully through valleys and plains. This was clear and fast-flowing water that swirled rapidly around giant boulders.

Seth spent some time looking for a place to cross and finally chose a spot where there were fewer dangerous rocks. Kneeling beside Dog, he said, "I am worried, old friend. I know you are not fond of water."

Dog whined softly and put his head on Seth's knee. Seth sighed and stood up. A grove of young saplings grew near the river. If he could cut them down and lash them together, perhaps he could use them to float across. The rest of the morning was spent felling several young trees, not an easy task with only a stone knife and ax. Still, by early afternoon he had them stripped of branches and laid side by side on the ground. Then he carefully selected strong but flexible vines to hold the wooden poles together. He supplemented these ties with all the leather rope strips he had in his pack.

When he finally stepped back to admire his work, he was pleased. Before him was a crude but fairly sturdy raft. Without hesitation, he threw on his pack—with his spear and walking stick securely strapped to it—and called to Dog.

Gingerly Dog stepped on the raft. Seth laughed. "It is either this or swim, my friend."

Swallowing his own fear, Seth pushed the tiny boat into the water. When it immediately started to drift downstream, he realized his mistake. He had forgotten to bring something to guide the raft, and now the current was too strong for him to push it back onshore. Desperately his eyes searched the bank. There was nothing. Then he remembered his spear. Pulling himself up, he freed the spear from its ties and plunged the end into the water, poling against the current. He had greatly miscalculated the strength of the river. For every inch he gained, the water seemed to pull him downstream another two. The water roared around him, and Seth was certain the vines would snap under such pressure. He was soaked with spray and his own sweat as he fought for balance on the heaving raft.

The roaring sound that once had sounded so far in the distance was louder now, almost like the thunder of a summer storm. Thunder! Suddenly Seth knew he was in terrible danger. He strained to see ahead, forgetting for a moment to steer with his makeshift oar. In that second the spear hit a rock and was wrenched from his hands. The raft began spinning, hurtling out of control. Dog, even more frightened, tried to stand up, but a sudden lurch threw him over the side into the foaming water. As Seth reached for him, he heard a sickening crunch, and he, too, was swept overboard.

Instantly he was sucked under and his body tumbled, tossed like a leaf, into some rocks. There was a pain in his chest and the bitter taste of fear in his throat. Then his head burst through the water, and there was a chance for one quick gulp of air before he was sucked under once more. The river dashed him about, and he felt a sharp pain. He was sure that he was going to die, though instead of sorrow he felt only surprise that it had come on such a beautiful day, with so little warning. Again and again his body was bounced on the rocks, and finally he felt himself falling down in a thundering rush of water.

Then suddenly all was calm, and his head was out of the water. He held on to a jagged rock, gulping life-giving air into his broken body.

"Dog," he screamed, looking wildly around. But he saw no speck of brown anywhere.

The water was red with blood near his leg. Weakly Seth pushed himself toward the land. Amazingly, his pack floated by, and he grabbed for it just as his feet touched river bottom. The ties that had held the walking stick dangled empty. Seth sank to his knees on the stony beach, using the last of his strength to drag his pack out of the water. Then he felt himself surrender to a darkness that was deeper than sleep.

The Lion

When Seth awoke, it was night, and he was shivering. He knew he should move, build a fire, and tend to his wounds. Each time he tried, his body shook with cold, a piercing pain shot through his side, and he could not find the courage to stir.

Groaning, he twisted so that he could see the river. He was below the falls now, but still close enough to hear the rumble and feel the spray. The falls were wide, though not very high. Even so, the water fell with a mighty force. He rolled slowly the other way. Only a few feet away, the trees grew thick and twisted with vines. He remembered what Abed had told him about this land being the home of lions. In the dark, the forest seemed mysterious and frightening.

Seth's fingers reached for the amulet around his neck. It was still there, wet but not lost. Furiously he jerked it off and threw it into the water. It had not brought him good fortune. He had made his own fate. Because of his stupidity, Dog was dead, and he would be, too.

That fearful thought gave him enough strength to crawl to the protective cover of some trees. There he listened carefully to the forest sounds. Every rustle of leaves or creak of a branch made him imagine the danger the thick growth might be hiding. Then, over the roar of the falls, came a noise he knew was real. Something was moving along the bank, stalking him. He heard it sniffing, following his scent, coming closer. Seth clutched at his bow, still tied to the pack. But before he could loosen it, something leaped, covering him with wet, happy licks.

"Dog," Seth whispered, hugging the animal in spite of its wet fur and his own pain. "You are alive. I am not alone."

Joyfully whining, Dog lay beside him. Twisting painfully to one side, Seth put his arm over Dog, and again he slept.

During the night, Seth developed a fever, and images passed in his mind like a series of dreams. One time he thought he was covered in warm robes, and he even imagined a fire. Then it seemed he was tended by gentle hands that wrapped his side in strips of leather and packed a cool poultice of leaves on his leg. He was sure there were times of sun, and others of darkness, and sometimes it seemed as though someone was forcing him to drink something warm and soothing.

Finally he opened his eyes and knew that he was better. Esu smiled down at him. "Aaa-eee, I am glad to see you."

"I thought you were a dream," Seth said, surprised by his weak, croaky voice.

"I am not a dream. I have been here for three days. Here, pinch me—see if I yell." Teasingly Esu held out an arm for Seth to touch.

"But why are you here? How are you here?"

"I knew you couldn't get along without me. Didn't I tell you that you would get lost or hurt? 'Esu,' I told myself, 'your brother is a great thinker. However, he is clumsy and not always practical.' I came back to where I left you, the next day. It took me that long to think about how stubborn and mean I was, I am sorry to admit. The city will be here other days, I told myself, but your brother may not. By the time I retraced my steps, though, you were already gone. I have followed you for days, but you always moved so fast I couldn't catch up. I was too far away to help when you went over the falling water. I walked downstream and crossed past the falls, where the water is smooth. I found you there." He shrugged.

"I owe you my life," Seth said.

"Could I do less for my brother? Now sleep, grow strong. We still have a long journey. Someday, though," he said with a grin, "you and I are going to find that city."

This time it was a restful sleep, and when Seth awoke, his head was clear and he was hungry. He looked around. Esu had made a shelter, with some skins stretched over the brush. Dog sat by the dying embers of a fire, and his tail wagged at the sight of Seth.

Esu crouched by a rabbit he had snared. "Good, you are up. I was just going to cook this rabbit. I wish you would hurry and get well. You are much better at this than I."

"Then you had better feed me before I starve and you have to do all your own cooking," Seth said, laughing. He used Esu's spear to pull himself up.

"I found your walking stick," Esu said cheerfully as he worked. "It is a little scratched. . . ." His voice faded as Dog leaped to his feet, his hair bristling and his teeth bared. From his throat rumbled a ferocious growl.

From the forest came an answering roar, and suddenly a huge lioness burst into the clearing. Dog leaped out to meet her, and for an instant there was a snarling tangle of fur and teeth. But Dog was no match for the lioness. Seth knew that it was only to protect him that Dog had challenged the great cat. He gripped his spear, looking for a chance to throw. Out of the corner of his eye he saw a shocked Esu, still crouched beside the rabbit. With a cry, Seth rushed at the lioness, stabbing her with all his strength. The lioness stumbled. Seth stabbed her again. This time she fell and did not get up.

Sobbing, Seth ran to Dog, forgetting about his own pain. "Dog, you can't die now!" he cried.

"Here, help me," Esu said, moving at last. "If we stop the bleeding, perhaps we can save him."

Together they tended Dog, washing his wounds and packing them with mud. Dog weakly licked their hands in thanks.

Finally Esu rocked back on his heels. "I think he will be all right." Then, turning to Seth, he said seriously, "You have killed a lion. That makes you a great hunter. Even Grunn will respect that."

There was a crashing in the brush, and for one dreadful moment Seth thought the lioness had a mate. He was much relieved to see two young men from the Goat People burst into the clearing.

As they shared the rabbit with Seth and Esu, the hunters told their story. The lioness was an old one, and she had attacked several people in the village. The two men had been following her for days.

"Will you come back with us?" one of them asked.

Seth shook his head. "We have decided to return to our own people. Tell Abed I will try to bring them to him."

The hunters exchanged a look. "Traders from the

big water came the day after you left. They said the mountain near the Lion People breathes fire and smoke, and it makes the ground tremble. The mountain spirits are angry, the traders told us."

"What about our people?" Esu asked. "Where did they go?"

"They are still in the cave. The traders say the Leader will not leave it. He says they are safe there." The hunter shrugged. "Maybe he is right. The Keeper-of-Magic agrees with him. But I would not want to live there."

Volcano

Now they had reason to hurry, but with Seth and Dog both wounded, progress was slow. Seth was frustrated and irritable, and would have walked on until he dropped. However, Esu insisted they keep an even pace and stop every night for rest.

"How can it help our people if you die before we get there?" he asked reasonably.

"I'm better now," Seth said. He winced slightly as he moved.

"If you won't take care of yourself, think of Dog," Esu complained mildly. "Besides, I don't think it is far now. A few more days and we should be able to see the hills."

Esu's voice was so firm that Seth had no choice but to listen. He knew Esu was right about Dog. Although he faithfully padded along beside him each day, the animal had not regained his strength. The bouncy exuberance had disappeared, and he never ventured ahead. At night, Dog fell into a deep sleep and hardly moved until morning.

As they made camp on the third night after the attack, they heard wolves in the distance. Dog's ears pointed up, and he raised his head to listen. "I wonder if he gets lonely for his own kind," Esu said.

"He liked the Goat People's dogs well enough," Seth said. "But he was so young when his mother died. Perhaps he thinks he is human like us." Some of the good humor was back in his voice.

"He is very restless. I wonder if it is the wolves or something else."

"What do you mean?"

"Do you smell anything unusual?" Esu asked.

Seth sniffed the night air. There was a faint, sharp smell. Then, when the wind shifted, he could smell nothing but earth and trees.

"Do you think it is the mountain spirits?"

Esu shrugged, but he looked uneasy. Dog prowled restlessly, pausing now and then to lift his nose in the air.

"We had better sleep lightly tonight," Esu said. He threw another log on the fire and wrapped himself in his robes. In a few minutes he was snoring so deeply a herd of bison could not have awakened him. Dog sat close to Seth, awake and alert, as if he knew something was wrong.

Seth awoke with the first rays of the sun. He was surprised to see that Esu was already up, staring at the mountain peaks near the cave. Seth crawled out of his robe and rubbed his eyes. There were clouds of gray smoke curling toward the sky, hiding the top of the mountain. When the wind moved the gray curtain, he could see a bright ring of red.

"All we have to do is cross that valley, and we will come to the hills and home," Esu said.

The earth shook beneath their feet. It was light and quick, over almost before they felt it. But the boys exchanged frightened glances, and Dog howled. It was a long, eerie sound in the silence.

Without speaking, they ate quickly and started off. Dog followed, but he seemed reluctant. Several times he stopped, and Seth had to coax him on. There was a tightness in the air that didn't match the clear blue sky, and the acrid smell grew worse.

"Listen," Esu said when they made camp that night.

Seth paused. "I don't hear anything."

"That's it. It is too quiet. I don't even hear a bird."

The next morning the two boys were up before dawn, grimly determined to finish their journey that day. They could see the hill that was home to the Lion

People, and the angry mountain looming just behind. Several times they felt trembling under their feet, and the sun was continually hidden with thick gray smoke. As they started the climb to the cave, they noticed a fine white ash covering the brush like a dusting of snow.

They managed to reach the ledge without being seen. Usually at this time of day, they would have passed hunters or women gathering food, but today they found everyone huddled around the entrance to the cave.

Mara saw them first. "It's Seth and Esu," she screamed, jumping up. Seth was alarmed to see how frail she looked.

Grunn stepped forward. He, too, was very thin. "Why have you returned with a beast to bring more bad fortune?"

Quickly Esu pulled the lion skins from their packs. He wrapped his around his shoulders and tucked Seth's around him.

"We have come as mighty hunters who have each killed a lion. We claim the right to be heard."

At the sight of the lion pelts, an excited murmuring went through the tribe. Several small children boldly reached out and touched the skins, and Seth saw Jontu's proud look. Now it was his turn. Everything depended on how well he said what he had to say. Seth glanced at Dog, sitting faithfully at his side, and took a deep breath.

"This animal did not bring bad fortune. The herds

have listened to the voice of the mountain spirits and moved away, as we must. There is a place," he said, "where the Lion People could make a new home. This place has golden hills of grain as far as the eye can see, and the river is wide and smooth. The hunting is good, but even when it's not, the people always have meat because they keep animals and kill only what they need."

"This is our home," Nar shouted. "He knows he is not wanted here, so he tries to trick us away from our cave. The mountain spirits will not harm us. Marnak has worked his magic to protect us."

The Lion People exchanged bewildered looks. This was One Leg, always alone and quiet. Yet here he stood in his lion skin, proudly, speaking boldly as any leader. A few turned away, but most listened.

Seth spoke again. "I think you are in great danger here. The mountain—"

"We are not in danger," Grunn interrupted stubbornly. Seth thought he heard desperation in his voice.

"The game is gone because of the picture maker," Marnak said. "He stole the good magic from the Lion People."

"His pictures are not magic," Seth shouted over the angry mutters. "They are only things of great beauty. I speak the truth. I ask only that you listen."

At a signal from Grunn, Nar picked up his spear and started toward Seth, but Jon-tu stepped between them. "We will hear what he says. Then we will decide." Something in his manner made Nar back away, and he looked helplessly at his father.

"We will listen," Grunn said, turning it into a joke. "I am in the mood for a good story."

So Seth began. He told them of the journey and the gentle Goat People, of Abed, Grandmother, and Sari. He told them of the wonders he had seen, which could be theirs. When he spoke of Sari, who ruled with her husband, Grunn snorted, but the women looked interested. So he spoke to the women, telling them about the pottery, the soft cloth woven from a plant, the beautiful jewelry. Last, he told them of Dog, his companionship and loyalty. He told how Dog had hunted for them, and how he had fought to save his life. It was after dark when he finished, and the blazing ring around the mountain was plainly visible, a fiery warning against the night sky.

"I say we follow this lion killer to the home of the Goat People," Jon-tu said. "I know him well, and he speaks only truth."

"I agree," said Sela. He held his arms protectively around his wife and children.

Seth flashed them a grateful smile, but Grunn stood up and pointed to Seth. "You know this boy. He was good for little. He only helped the women; now he wants us all to be women—to tend goats and grain. We are hunters," he roared, holding up his spear. "My son will fight this miserable dog person. He will drive him from the Lion People."

Nar stepped out of the crowd, holding his spear. His

face was split by a mocking grin, but his eyes were filled with hate.

"I will fight for Seth," yelled Esu, jumping between them.

The Lion People leaned forward eagerly, waiting to see what would happen. Some shook their heads, knowing that Seth could not win.

"Wait," Seth said. "I know that Nar is a great hunter. But is strength all that you require of your leader? If I prove that the things we have learned will make us stronger as a people, and not weaker, will you follow me?"

The people murmured, curious now. "What will you do?" Jon-tu asked.

Seth looked around. So much depended on the next few minutes. Here were the people that he had once thought hated him. Yet he could see in their eyes that most of them wanted him to win. He pointed to a faraway tree. "We will have a contest. Nar will throw his spear, and I will use this new weapon I was given by the Goat People. It will prove that the things I learned will make us stronger." He took his lion skin from his back and handed it to Esu. "Hang it from the tree, my brother."

"No one could throw a spear that far," Nar said. He stared at the bow and little spears. "Most certainly not with those little spears," he added scornfully.

"Then you agree to the contest? Whoever gets the closest wins."

Nar hesitated. He had been looking forward to beating Seth. But he knew from the mumbling that some would think such a fight unfair. Perhaps this would be even better. Seth would look like a fool. He glanced at his father, who shrugged. "I agree," Nar said.

Esu had reached the tree and hung the lion skin over a branch. He ran back, panting, just as Nar picked up his spear.

Nar's eyes narrowed, sizing up the distance. He pulled back his arm and braced his feet. His arm flashed forward, and the spear flew through the air, landing just short of the target. He turned to Seth with a triumphant grin.

Seth saw Jon-tu's worried face. It had been a magnificent throw. He saw Mara, sad but hopeful, and he smiled. He took careful aim, pointing the little spear up as Abed had taught him. With all his strength he pulled back on the bowstring, and a gasp went through the crowd. The arrow sailed through the air. Even from that distance, it was plainly visible, caught straight through the lion skin. Nar stared in disbelief.

"It is some kind of trick," he shouted. He picked up a knife and charged at Seth.

"No!" Grunn's voice roared. Nar stopped. With the knife still raised, he turned and faced his father.

"You agreed. Seth won fairly. You will not dishonor me."

Nar's arm dropped, and the knife fell from his fingers. Then suddenly Seth was surrounded by cheering people, excitedly making plans for the move. Dog barked happily at the noise, and several hands reached hesitantly to touch him. Seth saw Mara and took her hand. He looked at Ali to see if she was angry, but she smiled.

"Take only what you can carry," Seth said. "It is a long walk to our new home, and we must leave now. We will rest when we are far away from the mountain spirits."

As the people lit torches and packed their meager possessions, Seth looked at the burning mountain and then closed his eyes. Perhaps the spirits would grow angrier, raining fire and destruction down on the cave. Or perhaps they would sleep again as they had in the past. It no longer mattered. He could see the journey in his mind, the long line of Lion People making their way through the hills to the pleasant valley of the Goat People. Grunn and Nar would be shamed and refuse to go. But he would go to them and ask them to come. He would explain that the new life needed strong hands. There would be a place for everyone. He could imagine his people living together, learning new things, building together. Someday they would build a city where others could come and learn. What a tale that would be. But that, he thought, and smiled to himself, would be another story, for another day.